Truth Runs Deep

Sheila Callaham

Cover by Todd Coats

Copyright © 2011 by Sheila Callaham

Published in the United States of America.
ISBN: 978-1-936934-01-0
ISBN: 978-1-936934-00-3 (ebook)

www.truthrunsdeep.com
www.sheilacallaham.com

Dedicated to the memory of
my paternal grandmother,
Gladys Callaham

PREFACE

When I was a little girl I frequently walked around with a pad and pencil, scribbling out poems and the beginnings of stories that reflected my observations. I still remember my first official reading, a poem recited for my fifth grade English class:

Bee, bee,
Please little bee
Just g-g-go away and don't sting me.

I'll tiptoe slowly,
If you'll just stand by
And sting someone else when they walk by!

Although I have many stories in my head, it has taken me a long time to complete my first work of fiction. What prompted me to finally get on with it? A deep calling and the support and encouragement from some very important people in my life; especially Kyle and Tina Ross who encouraged me to finish what I started.

I'd like to thank the teachers who influenced my early years: the late Martha Caldwell, my fifth grade English teacher who first saw my way with words; the late Sue Hollis, who nurtured my love for science; the late Carol Hodges, who accepted my mathematical challenges and simply looked out for me when I was lost; and Carolyn Thomas who, during my last three years of high school, never stopped pushing me to read and write.

Fast forward to the last few years and I find myself still surrounded by wonderful people who have nurtured and supported my dreams, like my long-time friend and biggest cheerleader Glenna McGraw. I'm forever grateful to Dr. Jack Modell, the first to read my completed manuscript and encourage me to share it with others; Tamara Burkett and Janet Portzer, whose proofreading skills I am grateful; Dara Richardson, whose African American perspective ensured cultural authenticity; and Annette Byrd, an incredible woman whose dog Calvin was the inspiration for the dog in this book.

Other wonderful friends who shared their time to read and give feedback include Marty St. Clair, scientist extraordinaire; Dannibeth Farnum, an ever-so-talented creative; Theodore Furman, who always makes me feel like my contributions are important; Ken Gray and David Irlbeck, both who helped influence the development of my younger characters. I also want to acknowledge the many contributions from my copy editor, Richard Krawiec.

The Catholic Church is a complicated entity and I am grateful to Bill Irlbeck and former priest Jim Hynes for their insight and input.

I am eternally grateful to my family for indulging me precious weekend and vacation time over the past couple of years so that I could write, rewrite and write some more. I'm especially moved by the constant endorsement from my son Nathaniel Gay who, in addition to being my computer technology expert, has always been the voice beside me saying, "Yes, you can!"

Finally, my deepest love, appreciation and respect for my husband, Tom Bishop. It is through his committed love and support that I was able to see this through.

...pain is the breaking of the shell that encloses your understanding.

Kahlil Gibran

CHAPTER ONE

Police chief Carl Johnson was trained for instantaneous response, regardless of the circumstance or, in this case, the time. So when the phone rang at 0235 he answered it before the end of the first ring.

"Chief Johnson, this is Corporal Burke. I'm the dispatcher on duty, sir. Looks like we have a family wasted over on Mimosa Crescent. It's bad." The dispatcher paused.

Chief Johnson felt his gut tighten. Murder was never pretty and no matter how many times he got called to a scene, nor how high he built his emotional walls, death had a way of spooking him. He inhaled deeply and then exhaled into the phone. "I'm on my way. Give me the address."

He tried to leave the house as quickly and quietly as possible, hoping not to wake Tanya. But she was, after all, the wife of a long-time police officer and after eighteen years of marriage, she woke before the end of the first ring too.

"Where you going, baby?" she asked, turning on the lamp.

"How come I'm the only man that can't get out of the house

without his wife knowing? I'll never be able to live the double life I've always dreamed of," he chided.

"Uh-huh. Okay funny man, what time will you be home?"

Chief Johnson picked up his keys from the dresser and moved to sit next to Tanya. "It's going to be a long day, baby," he said, his voice serious. "I'll call you this afternoon to check in."

Tanya knew the routine and she knew by his tone that whatever happened was bad. "Okay. Love you."

"Love you, too" he said, leaning over to kiss her forehead before heading out.

Within five minutes, his patrol car was on Highway 64 headed to the beltway. Chief deliberately avoided thinking about what lay ahead. He focused instead on the night. Traffic was minimal. The moon was bright at a half-crescent in the clear sky above. With his windows open, the night was perfect. Perfect for murder.

He turned his car onto Powhawtan Parkway, named after the powerful Indian tribe that gave early Virginia settlers a run for their money in more ways than one. Moments later, Chief Johnson slowed to make a right onto G Street and then an immediate left onto Mimosa Crescent. He drove into what appeared to be a thousand flashing lights.

CHAPTER TWO

Father Richard William Cameron pushed back his chair, stood and picked up a glass of cranberry juice and the morning newspaper from the breakfast table. He could hear the house cook, Margaret, rattling pots and pans in the kitchen as he made his way down the dim hallway decorated with pictures and certificates, most of which were gifts from his loving congregation. Making a left into the formal sitting room, he stood before the French doors leading into his private study. Tucking the folded paper under his arm, he opened the left door, spun deftly around and backed into the room pulling the door with him. Just for that moment, he imagined himself the graceful Gene Kelly, gliding across the dance floor. It was the closest thing to a dance step he could do.

Like any priest, his study was a second sanctuary. Of the four walls that now enclosed him, one was a wall of windows—small panes that started low and reached almost to the ceiling 18 feet above. He often wished he could replace the small panes with larger ones to open the view to the modest garden; but that was extravagance on his part. This house – and all that came with it – was extravagant enough for a humble Catholic priest.

Two walls were floor to ceiling bookshelves containing his personal library. The wall connecting the study to the rest of the house was adorned with an original oil of red roses in a crystal vase and a set of English hunting scenes. The paintings, which framed the French doors, were signed "LegA" and had come with the house. He had never bothered to research the artist, but often admired the beauty of the work and he couldn't imagine ever having them removed.

Two dark brown leather chairs sat facing his desk. They were the soft, subtle Italian leather, stitched tightly in the seams rather than the hard leather folded under with brass tacks that he hated so. As Father Cameron saw it, these chairs invited visitors to make themselves comfortable; and, if a visitor was comfortable, he believed them more likely to speak from their spirit.

The large, stately mahogany desk had a rich, brown patina. It came with the house, as had most of the furnishings. Being a neat man, he kept little on the desk; only a legal-sized leather-bound writing pad and whatever books he was reading at the time. In the center drawer he kept his writing implements and stationery.

Two larger drawers to the left held his personal files and the drawers to the right were designated for his flirtation with art. There he kept various drawing pads, mechanical pencils, brushes, acrylic paints and small canvases. When the mood hit him, he would reach for his pad and sketch charcoal drawings of distant, solitary images; sometimes a gate partially open with no sign of anyone coming or going; sometimes a field with wildflowers growing madly in one area while the other part of the scene remained empty.

The office was large by clergy standards, but then so was his house. An old but impressive home, with more rooms than any Catholic priest could ever need, it was painted white with gray roof tiles. The front porch, large and refined, had gray painted floor boards anchoring four large white colonial columns. It was not a typical house for the street; in fact, it looked rather out of place surrounded by row houses occupied by middle-class families. But then the woman who willed it to the church was rather out of place as well.

Louisa Armstrong had been born and raised in the Deep South and a plantation home was her only idea of a real home. Her husband, eighteen years her senior and a successful businessman, had it built for her as a wedding gift and she had lived there until her death eight years earlier.

What seemed odd to Father Cameron was that neither Louisa nor her husband, who had died of a heart attack just two years before her own passing, had been Catholic. Nevertheless, her will explicitly stated that the house and property would go to St. Mark's for the sole purpose of housing its clergy.

The Catholic Church didn't ask questions – why look a gift "house" in the mouth? Naturally, the church officials were most pleased. The house, which sat less than two blocks from the church, was quite an addition to the small list of St. Mark's assets. The original clergy house, a tiny abode that stood right behind the church, had since been remodeled and was now a nursery and classrooms.

Father Cameron was gazing out the window when the phone

beckoned him to service. He turned slowly, scowled, and placed the paper and juice upon the desk as he moved around to sit. Only then did he answer.

"St. Mark's, Father Cameron speaking."

"Rick, this is Steve. Have you seen this morning's paper?" Father Cameron heard the voice of Stephen Mario, a friend from seminary who was the rector of Joseph's not more than five miles away. His voice was strained and he sounded as if he were gasping for breath.

"No, Steve, I've just come into my study. Why, what's wrong? You sound distraught."

"Just look at the paper, Rick. My God, I cannot believe. Please tell me I am dreaming," his voice cracked, as though fighting back sobs of despair.

Father Cameron reached for the folded paper and quickly scanned the front page. In a moments' time his eyes rested sadly on a family photo. The headline above read: **Family Murdered, No Suspects**

"Did you know the family?" Father Cameron asked gently, knowing already by Father Mario's voice that he did.

"Yes, they were mine," he said, his voice cracking with emotion. "He was a lay minister and she taught Sunday school. All three of their children, Michael, Patrick and James, were altar servers." He took a deep breath and then almost shouted at Father Cameron, "Rick, you know what this could have been..." his voice broke off.

Father Cameron shifted in his chair. Without even thinking, he turned to look at the drawers on the left of his desk. When he spoke, his words were carefully chosen.

"Steve, let us not jump to conclusions..." He paused for a moment, searching for the right words. "We've discussed this with the Bishop at great length and he firmly believes that we should not give any further attention to the matter. We all agreed that taking the issue public would only make matters worse."

Father Mario was trying to speak but the words escaped him. All he could think of was a few months back when little James celebrated his first Eucharist. In his mind, he saw them all as if it were yesterday. James looked like an angel; Carol and Allen looked so proud sitting in the pew with Michael and Patrick. Father Mario remembered Patrick making fun when James made a face after drinking from the chalice. A thought that previously made him smile now put him into deep despair.

He felt helpless and angry. He wanted revenge on Satan himself for reaching into his congregation and mercilessly conspiring against an innocent family. He felt a nagging suspicion for whom, or more precisely what, was behind the murders. Father Cameron was speaking again but Father Mario didn't hear him. He dropped the phone onto the bedroom floor as a sudden wave of nausea sent him running into the bathroom.

Father Cameron waited patiently until his friend returned. After a short-winded apology, Father Mario managed to gasp a few words of nonsense and question himself as to how he could manage the funeral services when he was as guilty of their murder as was anyone else. Father Cameron listened without speaking. When Father Mario paused, Father Cameron spoke calmly and evenly.

"Steve, you share no guilt in this crime. You will disassociate yourself from any memory that leads you to believe anything to the contrary. Now, I will be over in the next 10 minutes and we will sit down and talk through services."

"No, I just need some time to think, Rick. Really, I just need some time to think. I'll call you in a couple of hours, when I'm ready."

Father Cameron breathed heavily. Although they had gone to seminary together, Father Mario was 20 years younger than he. *And still emotionally young* he thought as he offered to call the Bishop on Father Mario's behalf before saying good-bye.

Regardless of the age difference, Father Cameron was attached to Father Mario. His heart went out for his friend's loss and for the fact that Father Mario somehow felt responsible. His eyes gazed again at the photo on the front page of a smiling family before turning again to the file drawer. He reached down, opened the lower drawer and pulled an unlabeled file from the back. He placed the file in the center of his desk and stared at it. He wondered if he focused hard enough on the file if he would be able to discern the truth behind it. Was it some hoax or was it a real threat to the Church? Surely, if it was valid, Bishop Grogan would have reacted differently.

Finally, he opened the file and began sifting through the papers. He wasn't reading them as he turned the pages. In fact, he wasn't really looking for anything. A chill ran down his spine, and he felt a sudden anger well up from the depths of his soul. He was a man of the cloth, he reminded himself, yet one could despise evil and the contents of this folder were clearly evil.

CHAPTER THREE

Sergeant Thomas Walker looked around the room as if divining some hidden clue. In reality he was trying to get a grip on himself. He had been on the Hampton police force for five years, but he would never be able to accept the horrors of the world. Other officers took it in stride, some even joked about the ingenuity of murder, but he could not do that. Nor did he want to. Sergeant Walker believed that for as long as he lived, he would remember the world was an evil place with the only safety to be found in the love of his family, country and God.

Sergeant Walker was shaking. He put his hands on his hips to steady the trembling and forced himself, once more, to remember how the bodies had been found earlier this morning. The coroner had removed them after his initial examination and now only red tape outlined where the death angel had appeared to claim its bounty – not once, but five times.

The Conner family had lived on Mimosa Crescent for three years. Active in the community, Allen Conner was a civilian working for the Department of Defense; his wife Carol stayed at home with their three boys aged seven, eleven and sixteen. The boys were all Boy Scouts, played basketball in the fall, baseball in the spring and Carol and Allen were always cheering them on from the sidelines.

This was a family built around church and community; now washed out of existence for no apparent reason. What was perfectly normal yesterday was now in shambles; an entire family eliminated from existence. It was more than Sergeant Walker could handle. He turned and rested his forehead against the wall, fighting back the emotions.

The house was crawling with people, outside reporters and camera crews shouted questions from behind the yellow tape. Two fellow police officers grinned and shook their heads as they watched Sergeant Walker wipe his eyes.

"There he goes again," Lieutenant Scott Marshall said under his breath.

"Well, like the old saying goes, if you can't stand the heat, get out of the fire," came the response from his partner.

"I think the man ought to stay behind a desk pushing papers, if you ask me."

"I just don't understand how he can be so good at something and be so bad at it at the same time." The two paused a moment as if pondering the meaning of the last statement before resuming their collection of hair and unidentified particles from the carpet near the front door.

"What do you men make of this mess?" It was the Chief, Carl Johnson, standing over them like a dark shadow. His skin was a shiny ebony, his eyes were like the night – revealing nothing as he hovered above his men like a hunter moving in for the kill. Though hard and relentless, he was a fair man who played by the book.

"Jesus, Chief, how do you do that? You're like some kind of stealth machine – coming up on folks without a sound," said one of the startled investigators.

In another situation, the Chief might have laughed and talked about the special ops training he received while in the military, but this wasn't a time for laughing. It had been a long morning since the call came in at 0235 this morning. He had spent the last several hours talking to the coroner's office, concerned neighbors and fighting off the press.

"Where the hell is Sergeant Walker?" he asked as he looked around to find him still leaning against the wall.

"Walker, get your ass over here now." Chief Johnson knew about Sergeant Walker's sensitivity but didn't allow it to interfere with his expectations. Sergeant Thomas Walker was the new kid on the block. *Claims he wants to be an investigator but turns soft at every crime scene.* Chief Johnson watched with furrowed brow as Sergeant Walker wiped his eyes with the back of his hand before turning toward the Chief.

"So, what do you think?"

"Best I can see, the attack was unexpected and quick," he answered. "Looks like the kids were killed first in their beds and the parents were awakened by the shots and came running out of their bedroom. Mr. Conner was shot while running down the hall."

"And, what about the wife? She was last?"

"Yes," Sergeant Walker answered, his voice wavering. "She was invited to die after the others were already dead or dying."

"What the hell are you talking about?"

"The killer or killers gave her the option of suicide and she took it."

"You mean she killed herself? Have you already heard from the coroner?"

"No, I don't need to talk to the coroner. Mrs. Conner probably had no choice, but she did kill herself."

"How can you be so sure that they didn't just put the gun in her hand when they were finished?"

"Because they were kind enough to put it all on video for us. A gift from the killers."

The Chief's face grew momentarily fierce before it softened again, his eyes betraying a moment of disbelief. "Let me see it."

CHAPTER FOUR

Father Cameron had accepted the role of pastor for St. Mark's eight years earlier. There were nine other Catholic churches in the area, including Father Mario's parish. It was not a large Catholic population, but proportionate in the grand scheme of practicing religions, with the exception of the Baptists, so long as you didn't categorize all the *other* churches as one church – the wrong one – as some faiths did.

Born and raised in Chicago, Father Cameron was a cradle Catholic. His mother was a homemaker, as most women in her community were. She raised seven children, four daughters and three sons. He was stuck in the middle. Lost in the flock, he hid from the responsibilities of the older siblings by avoiding getting too close to his mother's hand. He watched from a safe distance as she ran the household with an iron fist. Even his father submitted himself to the lady of the house when he returned from his job in the city as an accountant for a small brokerage.

He attended Catholic school, as did his siblings, taking the trolley twice daily to benefit from the tutelage of what he called the *mind-controlling nuns*. When he thought back to those days, he could do nothing but shake his head. '*What torment,*' he thought to himself. But the days of the nuns in their flowing habits and the long, hot days of summer, when his mother would drag them all to noon Mass every day of the week, confessions on Saturday, and Mass on Sunday, all blended into a childhood that was inconsequential.

He graduated a year early and went to the Catholic University of America, in Washington, DC, with a partial scholarship and the rest in school loans. It was there he developed his love for classical literature, reveling in the works of Shakespeare, Byron and Milton and graduating summa cum laude in English and Literature.

As nonchalantly as he had lived through his childhood, he passed through college. Day after day of quietly absorbing the basic drama of everyone else's life, he garnered very little for himself except a love for literature and philosophy. After graduation he traveled alone to Europe, living for six weeks on the meager savings he had managed while working part-time at the university and during his summers back in Chicago.

Arriving first in London, he rushed to Newstead to visit the birthplace of Byron and then to Stratford-upon-Avon to pay homage to Shakespeare. Eventually making his way to Paris, he spent weeks admiring works of art in the Louvre and wandering the side streets of Montmartre, once the famous hangout for Degas, Monet and Picasso. While in Paris, he met other Americans with whom he passed the time sketching idyllic cafe scenes while fantasizing about the passionate life of artists made famous through literature and works of fiction. The others he met –like him – came, longed for and left; none more an artist, though often more passionate.

His simplistic life came to a screeching halt when he accepted a job teaching English in a small high school in North Georgia. It was then that he believed his life found meaning – horrible and painful – but meaning, nonetheless. It was eighteen years later when he went to seminary, at the age of forty, and it was only then that his soul found peace.

And when the rain did stop
He looked from the prison gate
To see her smiling sweetly
She waved a delicate hand in the air
Where it lingered like a taunt—
He gathered his chains about him
And ran to where she was

When Father Cameron lifted his eyes to look out the picture window, they were moist from the memories. Thinking back to his North Georgia days always left his spirit darkened. He eased himself slowly from his chair, feeling suddenly very old, and gazed upon his shelves. He scanned the titles until his eyes rested upon a gardening book.

Although he loved gardens, he never had time to work outside. Margaret would occasionally weed the flowerbeds but what grew alongside the house and in the small garden did so without any human intervention. When Louisa planned her gardens, she had designed them with low maintenance in mind. Now he pulled one of her books from the shelf and flipped

19

through the pages.

The book seemed to open itself to the page of climbing vines and right before his eyes was the beautiful moonflower. In his mind, he could smell the white delicate flower as if the vine grew right in his study. But, in his mind he was still a long way from the safety of his home.

Fighting back the memories, he closed the book, placed it gently back on its shelf and turned to his desk. Staring him in the face was the headline that stirred a silent fear within him. He remembered that he needed to call the Bishop but he couldn't force himself to the phone. He thought again about the unlabeled folder in the back of his desk drawer and Father Mario's indication of a shared guilt in the murder of his own parishioners. He couldn't help but think of the innocent children.

"What would you do Louisa?" he said out loud to no one. He didn't know why he had said it, it just came out. He shook his head at his own surprise. "Getting old, I am." He picked up the phone and dialed the Bishop's number.

CHAPTER FIVE

Father Stephen Mario was not feeling well. After reading the front-page story about the Conner family, one of the most active families in his parish, he was blinded by a sense of guilt and raging anger. Without giving it so much as a second thought, he grabbed his keys and headed for the car. Unshaven and without his collar, he pulled out of the drive and turned the car in the direction of the Conner family home.

The neighborhood of Fox Hill was only a ten-minute drive from the rectory where he lived. As he drove he decided to focus on the living Conner family in the hopes that his thoughts would guarantee that, once he got there, it would all be a big mistake. He thought back to the parish picnic last fall. Carol had coordinated a potluck dinner that could have fed the entire church for a week. In his mind, he remembered the younger Conner boys falling all over each other in the three-legged race and Allen pushing so hard to get Michael to join the touch-football game. Father Mario knew why Michael didn't want to play, but did Allen?

Suddenly, Father Mario's mind flashed back to the morning paper and, though the details were scarce, he could see each of them lying lifeless in a pool of blood. Overwhelmed by the nightmarish vision, he almost drove off the road. Moments later, he was turning onto Mimosa Crescent and his eyes were immediately drawn to several women standing on the sidewalk, hands on the bars of their children's strollers. There were no smiles on their faces and they stared hard at him as he drove slowly by.

He could not drive any faster if he wanted. His speed was an indication of his anxiety for confronting the truth. He hoped with all of his heart that he would pull into the driveway, only to find that it was all a big mistake. That there was perhaps another family of the same name, perhaps another Allen Conner, Department of Defense civilian, member of some other church mistakenly identified as his own Conner family. He prayed to God and to the spirit of every merciful Saint for this to be a big mistake.

There was no mistake, however, for as he approached the Conner house he saw cars parked in the drive and on the curbs on both sides of the street; had it been a Saturday, one would have thought it was a big yard sale. But there were no yard sale signs, no tables out front, and no kids running around the yard looking for quarter toys.

Father Mario's stomach suddenly lurched and for a moment he felt lightheaded. He slowed the car and stopped in front of the house, marked off with yellow tape, trying to calm his mind. He wondered if they knew they were going to die. If they had time to be reconciled with God beforehand. He prayed that God would have mercy and hasten the family's entrance into heavenly glory.

He raised his head and looked in the direction of the house. Past the tape and through the bay window he could make out the figures of two men in conversation. One was waving his arms angrily about him, the other standing with hands on hips.

Nausea returning, he dropped his head onto the steering wheel and fought the wave of sickness that would not leave him. In his misery, he did not notice the police car that pulled up behind him. With cars parked on both sides of the curb, and Father Mario's car idling in the middle of the street, the officer could not maneuver around him.

At the sound of the siren behind him, Father Mario's whole body jumped. The officer had already stepped out of the patrol car and was walking toward Father Mario's open window.

"Good morning. You mind if I see your driver's license and registration?" the officer asked, bending down and shielding his eyes from the morning light reflected off the hood of Father Mario's car.

"Oh, good morning, officer," Father Mario stammered. "My name is Father Stephen Mario, I'm the rector of St. Joseph's Catholic Church and the Conner family were members of my parish."

The officer allowed Father Mario to finish his introductions, his ears only understanding that the Conners had been members at his parish.

"I'm sorry," the officer said after Father Mario finished speaking. "What was your name again?"

"Father Stephen Mario, rector at St. Joseph's Catholic church."

"Where's your collar, Father?" asked the officer. "I thought priests always wore that little white collar?"

"Oh, I must have forgotten it this morning officer," Father Mario said, reaching up to feel the spot where the collar normally formed stiffly around his neck. "I've been so stunned about all of this, I can't even think straight."

"I understand," the officer responded sympathetically. "How did you learn about the tragedy?"

"I didn't know until I opened the front page of the paper this morning. I guess it must have happened late last night but early enough that the papers picked it up," Father Mario was thinking, in his mind trying to put it all together, talking through the timing as he imagined it in his mind.

"Uh-huh, that's the way news works it seems," the officer responded, noting Father Mario's summation of the possible time of death.

"Father Mario, as a matter of procedure, I need to see your license and registration."

"Yes, of course," he said, reaching into his back pocket for his wallet from which he pulled his license. While the officer examined it, he leaned over to open the glove compartment and shuffled through a few papers until he found the registration.

"Thanks. Give me just a minute and I'll be right back."

Father Mario took a deep breath and looked out the windshield. A small crowd had gathered and stared at him from a distance, leaning into each other to speak behind hands held near their faces.

Suddenly it occurred to him that he might be considered a suspect. He looked at the crowd. It seemed each member in the group was staring at him with squinted eyes that were either combating the sun or drilling past the windows of the car to see

24

him more clearly. A few of them pointed. Father Mario then remembered from the movies he watched when he was growing up. *The murderer always returns to the scene.* Even the Book of Proverbs concedes this human behavior in chapter twenty-six: As a dog returns to his vomit, a fool returns to his folly.

Heavenly Father, what a day to run out without my collar! He looked again at the crowd, which suddenly appeared agitated, menacing. Here he was, a man of God, likely being considered a horrific murderer.

In the rearview mirror, Father Mario saw the officer talking on his radio. He looked from the rearview mirror, back to the onlookers, to the bay window of the Conners' house and then back to the rearview mirror. He felt a heightened sense of anxiety when he saw the officer returning with his license and registration.

"So Father Mario, what can I do for you this morning?"

For a moment, Father Mario felt stunned. He wasn't sure why he had driven to the Conner home; after all, what could he do to help? How could he serve in this circumstance? He was devastated by the loss of the Conner family. In his heart, he carried a dark fear that the Bishop had dismissed as nonsense. He'd been made to promise never to speak of it again. Even if he did break his oath and shared the incident, in confidence, it wouldn't be this way. He would insist on speaking privately to the Police Chief; he wouldn't bring anything up to this officer standing on the side of the street.

"I'm sorry officer; I'm just so stunned by all of this. I really wanted to confirm what I read in the paper. I guess I'd hoped that once I got here it would be a big mistake; but, I see it isn't."

"No, I'm afraid there is no mistake," the officer responded, as he watched the two plain-clothed agents approach the car.

"This is Father Stephen Mario," he told the men once they were standing beside the car. "He says that the Conners were members of his parish."

The two agents looked thoughtfully at Father Mario, unshaven, without collar and whose eyes appeared at one moment full of despair and pain and the next filled with anxiety and fear.

"Father Mario," said the shorter of the two, "my name is George Lacey. I'm a special investigator. Why don't you find a place to park; then we can speak privately."

Father Mario nodded in agreement and pulled his car slowly forward to park on the curb a few houses down from the Conners'. As he passed the small crowd gathered on the sidewalk, they moved away from his car but he felt their cold, hard stares pressing on him. Opening the door to get out, he suddenly realized how frightened he felt about death – this circumstance of death in particular. In a matter of moments, his fear had been confirmed. The Conner family, who he had loved and ministered to over the last several years, had been murdered. He had seen death many times before, but never in such evil dressing. And never someone so close to him.

Father Mario took a deep breath and turned to join the special agents who were waiting under a shade tree near the sidewalk. As he walked, his legs weakened and another wave of nausea made him grab his stomach as if trying to hold it in place. The crowd had moved to the far side of the street and continued their observation from a safer distance, as if fearful of him.

"You okay," investigator Lacey asked as Father Mario

approached. "You look a little sick."

"Yeah, I'm okay. I'm just really shaken by all of this, that's all," Father Mario replied as he extended his hand to go through the formalities of introductions.

"Don't you guys wear those little white collars all the time?" asked the taller, younger of the two men.

"Yes, yes, we do. I seemed to have left home this morning without putting it on," he said, reaching up again to feel where his collar should have been. He felt vulnerable and foolish.

CHAPTER SIX

Father Cameron was surprised when Bishop Grogan answered the phone. He expected to be greeted with the normal formalities of church protocol – the administrator would answer the phone, a message would be sent forward to inquire as to availability and most likely Father Cameron would be asked to make an appointment to speak with the Bishop. So, when the Bishop himself answered the phone, Father Cameron was not quite prepared to dive directly into the intimacy of the subject.

"Your Excellency, this is Rick Cameron from St. Mark's. I'm afraid I have some tragic news," he paused for the Bishop's permission to continue.

"Yes, Rick. May God have mercy, what is your news?"

"Our brother in the Church, Stephen Mario from St. Joseph's, has lost one of his parish families to what appears to be a brutal murder; an active husband and wife and their three sons. Father Mario is beside himself with grief, as can be expected."

On the other end of the line, Bishop Grogan dropped his head in silent prayer.

"May Almighty God have mercy on them, forgive them their sins and bring them to everlasting life."

"Amen," Rick echoed softly, crossing himself slowly.

"Rick, this is indeed tragic. Not only for the family and for Father Mario, but for the lost soul or souls responsible."

"Yes, that brings me to my next point," he hesitated while trying to pull the right words onto his tongue. "Father Mario fears that the murders might have been premeditated; perhaps resulting from the..." he hesitated, again fearing to say what Bishop Grogan had told them must never be repeated.

"No, Rick, let's not go there. There is absolutely no validity in that whatsoever. Steve needs to get his head around that. There will be absolutely no further discussion. I understand that Steve is feeling a great loss and most likely in a state of shock. But, he must not get carried away by his imagination. I shall call him straight away to offer my condolences as well as my reassurance that all will be well."

"Yes. Thank you for understanding."

"Of course, Rick. May the peace and love of the Lord be always with you."

"And also with you." Without a word more, he heard a soft click in his ear. The conversation was ended. He leaned back in his chair and sighed deeply only to remember that sighing was a coping mechanism. *Coping with what?* His moist hands were gripping the arms of his chair. *What is wrong with me? Why are my palms wet?* And, without realizing it, he drew in another deep breath only to exhale it in a long and deep sigh.

CHAPTER SEVEN

Alexander Grogan sat back in his chair after speaking with Father Cameron. He brought his hands together in prayer and dropped his chin upon them to rest. For a moment, he let his mind consider the trappings of Father Mario's concern before brushing it all aside and thinking about how best to redirect Father Mario's suspicions so that the subject could be put to rest once and for all.

He reminded himself of Father Mario's past – one that, like many others, was a story of escape. Born to high school sweethearts in the small, rural northeast Texas town of Quanah, Stephen Mario grew up wanting only one thing – to leave. In an area where three out of four residents never got beyond high school, it had been both a blessing and a curse that Father Mario was born with an intellect that exceeded those around him.

Bishop Grogan considered Father Mario's religious background. His mother had been a member of the First Assembly of God but his father never went to church. In fact, Bishop Grogan was fairly certain that Father Mario's father wasn't even in the picture from the time he was a young boy. According to Father Mario's telling of the story, although he had gone to Sunday school and church with his mother, he grew up feeling rather disconnected from God altogether. And, like most young adults, he went through a period of believing nothing at all.

It was Stephen Mario's brilliance that got him away from a small town mentality. As fate would have it, he left Quanah at the age of 17 to accept a full scholarship at Loyola University in Chicago. Knowing nothing about the Catholic Church, much less the Jesuit tradition that Loyola carried forth, Father Mario cared only that he would experience the excitement of city life and continued learning in a challenging environment.

Father Mario's conversion to Catholicism didn't happen right away but seemed an inevitable result of the friendships he'd built. When his best friend decided in his junior year to go on to seminary after graduation, Steve began to learn about the Catholic Church. In part, he wanted to understand what drew young men to such a rigid path. But, at the deepest level of his being, he was searching for something to fill his emptiness. Not only did he convert to Catholicism, he followed his friend to Mundelein Seminary. It was during a lecture series in his first semester that Father Mario first met Bishop Grogan. After the lecture, the student had approached Bishop Grogan to ask a question. One question turned into another and another, until the Bishop finally invited him dinner. It had been the beginning of an informal mentorship.

In Bishop Grogan's experience, converts to the Catholic Church were much more diligent about church laws. In this respect the Bishop thought he'd find the means to influence Father Mario. He picked up the phone to ask his secretary to place the call, but then remembered his secretary had called in sick. "So inconvenient," Bishop Grogan mumbled under his breath. He stood to move to the next room where his secretary should have been sitting. "Why is everyone else so susceptible to every bug that goes around?" he asked to no one in particular. Shuffling through papers and notebooks on the desk, he opened a couple of drawers looking through files. At last he found the file for St. Joseph's.

CHAPTER EIGHT

Police Chief Carl Johnson watched from the front bay window as Father Mario pulled his car to the curb and stepped out to speak to the investigators. His dark eyes squinted as he focused intently on every aspect of the man he saw walking toward the house. "Walker!" the Chief shouted over his shoulder. "Come have a look."

Sergeant Walker, who was writing in his notebook, immediately made his way across the foyer and into the front dining room where Chief Johnson was looking out the bay window.

"What do you make of this one?" he asked, his gaze still steady on Father Mario, who was going through the motions of listening attentively and then responding awkwardly.

Walker focused intently on Father Mario – reaching out to him in his mind. Walker's focus was not on what the man might be saying, but rather looking for signs that he might be leaving something out. He couldn't hear the conversation, but that wasn't important at this time. This was a read on body language.

Outside, Investigator Lacey and the younger agent had

positioned themselves so that, from the window, Father Mario's face could be clearly seen. Although Walker had a sense of something being not quite right in less than ten seconds, he didn't speak for a couple of minutes. He wanted to make certain of his intuition because he knew the Chief would waste no time in acting. Finally, he looked at Chief Johnson and answered, "I think you'll want to talk to him."

"That was my read as well," the Chief responded. "Bring him in."

"You mean, bring him into the house, or you want to see him back at the station?"

"In the house. Now."

"Yes, sir... uh, sir might that be a problem with," he cleared his throat softly, "forensics. This is, after all, a crime scene," his voice trailed off.

The Chief chuckled quietly to himself without even so much as looking at the young Sergeant. His gaze continued to rest on the conversation taking place outside. Sergeant Walker followed his gaze out the window before turning toward the front door.

From the top of the house steps, Sergeant Walker surveyed the landscape. Groups of neighbors stood watching, arms folded tightly over their chests. Standing under a large oak that shaded most of the front yard stood the three men that Chief Johnson had been watching. As he walked down the four brick steps and started across the yard, Walker could feel the Chief's eyes on him. Approaching the men, he heard Lacey talking about his grandmother's apple orchard.

"Sergeant Walker, glad you're here," Lacey said as he joined them. "This is Father Stephen Mario, rector of St. Joseph's

Catholic church where the Conner family belonged. He read about the tragedy in the morning news – damn press – I swear they must have our phones tapped."

"I'm sorry for your loss, Father," Sergeant Walker said with an extended hand. Father Mario offered a weak, moist handshake along with a nod to indicate acceptance of the condolence. For a moment the four men stood, saying nothing as they looked from one to the other. Lacey had rightly guessed that the Chief sent Walker out with a purpose in mind, so he waited patiently. The younger agent shadowing Lacey shuffled his feet nervously, not sure of what kind of psychological warfare was being waged.

Sergeant Walker, standing with his hands resting on his hips, had forgotten for a moment that the Chief's eyes were on him. He'd forgotten for a moment that he had been told to bring the man into the crime scene for questioning. Instead, he was caught up in watching Father Mario look from officer to officer, then over his shoulder at the neighborhood crowd, then down to the grass at his shoes before reaching his hand up to his neck where his collar should have been. Gestures screaming that this man was not only petrified, but that he was withholding something of major importance.

"So Walker, how are things going? Is Chief Johnson about wrapped up in there?" Lacey asked in an effort to prompt Walker into action.

"Yes," Sergeant Walker answered, bringing himself out of his trance. "But, I'm sure he'd like to speak to you, Father Mario, as the family priest. There might be some helpful info you could share in the case."

"I doubt I can offer any insight," said Father Mario, whose nerves were close to collapse. He had just spent the last ten minutes answering the occasional question about the Conners' church activities, while being subjected to the most mundane and unrelated tales of childhood woes from this George Lacey person, who claimed to be a special investigator. If George Lacey was the norm for this police department, there would be no hope for the Conner family, Father Mario had thought.

"We would be grateful for anything. I'm sure you will want whoever is responsible for this tragedy to be apprehended."

Father Mario nodded his head in agreement. Yet he didn't move from the spot under the tree where he'd been standing for the last ten minutes. Instead, he stared blankly at Sergeant Walker.

"This way please," Sergeant Walker offered, turning back toward the house.

All three men looked up at Sergeant Walker in surprise; still no one moved. Sergeant Walker's eyes met the Chief's before turning back to see that no one was following. "Father Mario, Chief Johnson is waiting for you in the house."

Suddenly Sergeant Walker thought he understood the Chief's intentions; Father Mario had just been asked into the Conner's home, but he had no way of knowing that the bodies had been removed from the home hours earlier. What Sergeant Walker couldn't get his head around was why the Chief would put the priest in this awkward position.

"Do you need to sit down?" Investigator Lacey asked reaching out toward Father Mario, who had swayed as if lightheaded. "You okay?"

"This way, please," Sergeant Walker echoed again, indicating the direction of the house with his outstretched arm.

In that moment, Father Mario's nostrils suddenly filled with the smell of incense and he found himself inside his church. He saw the Conner's oldest son Michael walking in front of him, gently swinging the brass thurible and filling the church with the fragrant smoke that symbolized their prayers being carried up to heaven. He never even felt his head hit the ground as his legs collapsed under him.

As Chief Johnson watched Father Mario's tall, thin frame fold itself up on the grass under the shady oak, he couldn't help but put his clasped hand up to his mouth to stifle a snicker. Oh, how he'd seen this one coming. He shook his head as he trotted out the front door, jumped the steps by twos and joined the men who by now were on all sides of Father Mario, trying to rouse him with slaps on the cheek.

"Good catch, men. First you scare him half to death and then watch him fall," said Chief Johnson, sounding brash even though he intended it half-heartedly. "Ever think of getting the salts out of the car?"

As the younger agent jumped up and headed for the car, Chief Johnson moved over to get a closer look at the still unconscious man. "So, what's the deal with this one? Who is he?"

"Father Stephen Mario, rector of St. Joseph's Catholic church. Priest to the late Conners family," Investigator Lacey recited back.

"Where's the collar?" asked the Chief. "I thought priests always wore a collar?"

"Ran out in a rush, all upset about the family after reading it in the morning press," answered the investigator.

"Damn press."

"My sentiments, exactly," Investigator Lacey echoed.

"Humph. I'm not sure I'm so comfortable sharing your sentiments," retorted the Chief, again intending jest but sounding full of sarcasm. "Let's try to sit him up, maybe that'll bring him out of his stupor."

Investigator Lacey grabbed Father Mario by the arm on one side and the younger agent straightened Father Mario's bent legs before grabbing him on the other. As they raised Father Mario to a sitting position, he winced in pain and immediately put his hand to the back of his head.

"Ouch, ouch, ouch, let me lay back down, please! My head is killing me," Father Mario pleaded.

"Well, at least he's polite," said the Chief.

"That's probably because he's a priest," retorted Lacey, still stinging from what he thought was the Chief's sarcasm toward him.

"I dunno, I've met some pretty rude church people," offered the young agent, with a laugh. "One of the reasons I don't go to church," he added.

Chief Johnson looked over at the young agent, a new recruit who had been shadowing Lacey for the last couple of months. Father Mario had sunk back into a semi-conscious state and was mumbling again about revealing evidence against the church.

"What do you make of this one? Zach, isn't it?" he asked the young agent.

"Yes, sir," Zach answered as he quickly considered his response. He was young and plenty ambitious, so he didn't think twice about offering up a few of the words he'd seen

Sergeant Walker scribble in his notebook as he stood over him a moment ago.

"It's possible that his mumbling indicates some sort of guilt complex although not necessarily directly related to the crime." Zach had strung that sentence together after reading the words *guilt complex* and *≠ crime*. He decided to elaborate, referring to his earlier observations during the discussion prior to Father Mario losing consciousness.

"He did seem nervous about something. Very odd behavior for a priest, I would think."

"Says the man with no religious affiliation," rebuffed Chief Johnson.

"I've done the church thing before, I've just elected not to do it anymore," Zach responded defensively.

"Okay, good enough. Let's call an ambulance and get him to the hospital. He might have a concussion which could account for the delirium," the Chief instructed. "Radio back to the station and have someone call St. Joseph's. We'll need to notify someone within the church, the Bishop, the Pope, whoever. Walker, are you done in the house?"

"I'd like just a bit more time to make a few more notes," Sergeant Walker said, casting a suspicious eye toward Zach, who had walked over to the police car to radio the station.

"Speaking of notes, do you mind if I have a look at what notes you took while our priest was on his back?"

Sergeant Walker looked at the scribbles on his pad before handing it over to the Chief, who looked at it briefly and then put his hand to his mouth to stifle another snicker. He looked at Sergeant Walker mischievously, "I didn't want to see your notes on Zach's comments. I wanted to know what *you* were thinking."

"This was what I was thinking," said Sergeant Walker, not hiding his irritation. "I swear he read my notes."

"Uh-huh, you just figuring that one out? Come on, let's wrap up here. I want to ride over in the ambulance with the priest. Take my car and meet me at the hospital. It should be an interesting afternoon."

CHAPTER NINE

As Father Stephen Mario lay on the ground looking up through the leaves of the oak tree, glimpsing the blue of the sky beyond, his mind raced. He was never sure from one moment to the next if he was in a bad nightmare or if he'd been injured in some car crash. All he knew with any certainty was that his head ached with a sharp pain every time he moved or tried to think. Instead, he lay on the soft, green grass and allowed his mind to go where it would – that hurt less than trying to control its navigation.

In the few minutes he lay there before hearing the sirens of the ambulance, he'd been eight years old and playing in the backyard of his parents' home; he'd been back to his first day in the seminary; he'd experienced for another time his first kiss; and he'd argued with Father Cameron for the umpteenth time about the file that he hid in the back of his lower file drawer on the left-side of his desk.

Drifting in and out of consciousness, Father Mario felt suddenly very alone and frightened as the paramedics placed him on the gurney and loaded him into the ambulance. Perhaps it was this overwhelming sense of loneliness that prompted him to open up to the black man who insisted on accompanying him to the hospital.

CHAPTER TEN

Bishop Grogan dialed the number for St. Joseph's expecting that Father Mario would be in the parish office. The phone was answered promptly by Sarah Pulley, the part-time parish administrator who, startled that the Bishop was calling, momentarily forgot that Father Mario hadn't yet come into the office. Putting him on hold, she half-ran to Father Mario's office before regaining her memory. As she turned to run back to the phone, it rang again. Thinking that she'd accidentally hung up on the Bishop, Sarah quickly switched over to the other line, offering apologies before even saying hello.

"Is this St. Joseph's?" a woman's voice asked.

"Oh, yes, I'm sorry," Sarah said. "I thought I was picking up the other line, can you hold please?"

"This is the Hampton Police Department. I need to report that Father Stephen Mario is being transported to Sentara Hospital."

"Father Mario is in the hospital? What happened? Will he be okay?"

"Yes, he collapsed, but the emergency crew who tended him

onsite said that he is in stable condition. Will someone be able to care for him when he's released?"

"Yes, of course," Sarah offered. "I'll notify our diocesan office right away. Thank you so much for the call."

As Sarah hung up, she saw the other line flashing and quickly picked up the Bishop's line to give him the news.

"Bishop Grogan, I'm so sorry for keeping you holding. I'm afraid I have some bad news."

For the second time in a short span of time, Bishop Grogan braced himself, this time expecting a repeat of the Conner family news. "Yes, go ahead."

"I just received a call from the Hampton Police Department to inform me that Father Mario is in the hospital. I don't know the details – all she said was that he'd collapsed and they wanted to make sure he had someone to care for him when he was released."

"Of course, I shall go myself to see that he's brought safely home and cared for," offered the Bishop, hoping to ease Sarah's concern as well as her curiosity. "Please be so kind as to call Father Cameron at St. Mark's and ask him to meet me at the hospital." Without even waiting for Sarah's response, he hung up the phone.

CHAPTER ELEVEN

Bishop Grogan entered the front doors of Sentara CarePlex Hospital and looked for the information desk. Since he had no idea what happened to Father Mario, he didn't know whether to go to the emergency room or ask for a room number at the information desk in the main lobby.

He hoped he would not run into any of the diocesan priests, as his visits to the area were always announced in advance. His sudden appearance would quickly spread and, given his position, he'd be invited to every parish activity in the area. He wasn't in the mood for that at the moment. Knowing the hospital chapel and chaplaincy office were on the main floor, adjacent to the lobby, he quickly scanned for signs of clerical activity. Seeing none, he proceeded hastily to the information desk.

The young, bright-eyed receptionist took the Bishop's request, quickly typed into the computer and then pointed him to the nearby elevator. She provided him a small slip of paper that read: Stephen Mario, room 523. He thanked her with a smile and nod.

As he walked toward the elevator, another concern came to mind. Knowing that the chaplaincy provided care to patients by request or referral, and knowing that hospital policy espoused contacting the chaplain's office if a patient expressed anxiety or emotional distress, he hoped that Father Mario had not demonstrated enough distress to warrant a clerical visit. The last thing Bishop Grogan needed was to encounter another priest with a face full of questions.

He could only imagine how apprehensive Father Mario might have been after this morning's news and the loss of an entire parish family. So long as Father Mario hadn't spoken to anyone else about his overzealous concerns, all would be well.

Bishop Grogan didn't like thinking about the topic that Fathers Mario and Cameron had brought to him last summer. The whole scenario seemed to him nothing more than a juvenile joke. Yet the two priests were clearly concerned and Father Cameron, whom he considered a level-headed theologian, was most sincere. Nevertheless, he had convinced them that their concerns had been noted and that the situation would be watched carefully. Then he had made it very clear that the topic was not to be mentioned again.

He recalled putting the folder of *evidence* they had given him in the back of his locked file drawer and realized that he had forgotten the whole episode until Father Cameron's call this morning. It wasn't just last year's discussion that prompted Bishop Grogan's immediate response to ensure Father Mario's care, there was a potential scandal brewing at St. Joseph's that the priest knew nothing about. It was a scandal that he was working feverishly to avoid. This morning's tragedy added a heartbreaking and ill-fated complexity that he would have to supervise closely.

His thinking, as he had made the ninety minute drive from his diocesan office in Richmond, was that he and Father Cameron would persuade Father Mario that this tragedy had nothing to do with him or what they had discussed last summer. Bishop Grogan knew Father Mario well enough – or so he thought – that he trusted his ability to influence the young priest.

The Bishop checked his watch as he felt the elevator hoist him up. He expected Father Cameron to be waiting for him in Father Mario's room and hopefully making progress toward easing the priest's fear-based emotions. What Bishop Grogan never anticipated, however, was walking into Father Mario's room to find Hampton Police Chief Carl Johnson.

CHAPTER TWELVE

For Chief Carl Johnson, the ride to the hospital with Father Stephen Mario was everything he'd hoped it would be and more. It was clear that the sad priest carried around a lot of emotional baggage and in this state of added distress, he provided a fountain of information. Chief Johnson listened sympathetically, nodded and uh-huhed at all the right times. He even held the priest's hand when sobs took over the story-telling, shaking the gurney on which the thin priest lay.

To Chief Johnson, this was not deceptive, not manipulative, not the least bit unethical. He was simply doing his job and Father Mario was making it a cakewalk. Although Father Mario was easy to read, the Chief knew he could often get people to say things they would never say to anyone else. In his mind, this unique gift was divinely inspired and his promise to his Maker was that he would only use it for good and not selfish purposes. Admittedly, that line was not always clearly defined; but in this case, an entire family had been ruthlessly murdered. Children shot in their beds as they slept. Who could do such a thing? Yes, he would do everything he could, without fail, to put a face and name to this tragedy.

By the time they arrived at the emergency room, Father Mario was oscillating between clear cognitive stability and consciousness, followed by emotional crisis and momentary black outs. One minute he would be answering the physician's questions about former head trauma and the next minute hospital staff would be reaching for more smelling salts.

For Chief Johnson, who now watched from the edge of the room, it was a painful place to be. He felt such angst coming from the priest that it evoked in him a deep sense of compassion that he used to immerse himself in Father Mario's pain. The technique and resulting experience helped Chief Johnson understand the priest. What he felt was an overwhelming sense of anguish and loss.

Sergeant Walker, who arrived moments after the ambulance, seemed to be in a similar trance, broken only when he would suddenly look away from the distraught priest to scribble notes in his little book.

After the physician concluded that Father Mario had suffered a mild concussion and diagnosed him with an acute level of anxiety and distress, he was moved to a private room at the request of Chief Johnson. Once settled, an IV was inserted into the vein of his left arm; the clear fluid dripping quickly. Soon, the distraught man was sleeping.

Chief Johnson settled into a chair next to Father Mario's bed and watched him as he slept. He considered the information he had gathered during the ten minutes spent with the priest in the back of the ambulance. Although occasionally nothing more than incoherent babbling, Chief Johnson had gathered enough information to conclude there were two people he needed to talk to right away. The Chief opened the bedside drawer and withdrew the phonebook. He flipped the pages and then ran his fingers down one of the columns. Finally he picked up the phone and dialed St. Joseph's.

Sarah Pulley answered on the first ring. "St. Joseph's Catholic Church."

"Good morning, Ms. Pulley. This is police chief Carl Johnson. I am hoping you can assist me or direct me to someone who can."

"Yes, sir, officer. How may I help you?"

"Well, I think you – or someone in your church – were already notified about Father Mario being in the hospital?"

"Oh yes, someone called me about a couple of hours ago. I've already notified Bishop Grogan. He's driving in from Richmond to take care of Father Mario. How is Father Mario doing? How did he end up at the Conner residence anyway? Goodness, I've called the hospital half a dozen times in the last hour trying to get an update on his condition."

"Father Mario came to the scene and it appeared to be too much for him but he is going to be fine. He's resting now. And, I'm so glad to know that Bishop Grogan will be looking after Father Mario. I'm surprised that the Bishop is taking on this responsibility himself."

"He also asked Father Cameron from St. Mark's to help out. They should both be on their way to the hospital as we speak."

"Is that Father Rick Cameron, by chance?" the Chief asked, hopefully.

"Yes, it is. Do you know him?"

"Just heard his name. I look forward to meeting them. You've been very helpful Ms. Pulley. Thanks again."

"Chief Johnson, before you go... I know you can't talk about the murder case, but this is such a tragedy for our parish. I just have to ask if you know that a number of members of St. Joseph's have filed a letter of complaint with Bishop Grogan asking for Father Mario's removal? Mr. Conner was co-leading that committee. I'm not trying to say that Father Mario would ever do anything like this..." she paused. "I guess I just want to know if you think other church members are in danger or if this is an isolated tragedy?"

Chief Johnson listened intently, as he focused on the face of the sleeping priest. His mind raced as he stitched together the information he had so far. He was racing against the clock to decipher possible suspects and motives. While Father Mario's mumblings pointed the Chief in one direction, Sarah Pulley's information now pointed him in another.

"Ms. Pulley, I don't think other church members need to be afraid. But could I set up some time to speak to you further about your concerns?"

Chief Johnson scribbled a few notes as he and Sarah Pulley confirmed her availability. It was going to be an interesting case.

CHAPTER THIRTEEN

When Father Richard Cameron returned to his parish office after noon mass, there was an urgent phone message waiting for him from Sarah Pulley at St. Joseph's. Not believing his ears, he replayed the message a second time.

Father Cameron, this is Sarah Pulley from St. Joseph's. I'm calling to inform you that Father Mario was taken to the Sentara Hospital around 11:00 a.m. I've called Bishop Grogan and he is on his way. He asked that I call you and have you meet him there. Please call if I can be of further assistance.

Father Cameron couldn't believe it. Father Mario was in the hospital and that he was to meet Bishop Grogan there. The message had been received at 11:43 and it was now 1:37. If it took the Bishop an hour and a half to make the drive, plus another 15 minutes or so to park and make his way through the hospital maze to Father Mario, then the Bishop had probably just arrived and would be waiting on him.

Father Cameron hurried out through the back exit to avoid any parishioners who might still be in the church. He considered calling the hospital to leave a message for the Bishop that he was on his way, but decided against it. Instead, he called St. Joseph's to see if anyone was tending the office. If so, he was hoping to hear details about what had happened.

Sarah Pulley answered the phone with a cheerful disposition – rather odd, given the circumstances, Father Cameron thought as he hurriedly walked the two blocks home to get his car.

"Sarah, this is Father Cameron at St. Mark's."

"Oh, Father Cameron, thank goodness. Are you with Bishop Grogan? How is Father Mario? I just can't believe all that has happened today – life can be so brutal."

Father Cameron suppressed the judgment that arose in him as he heard Sarah's voice change from cheer to dramatic concern.

"No, I'm not at the hospital as of yet, I just got out of noon mass. I should be there in about ten minutes."

"Oh dear, well you know that Bishop Grogan is probably already there and waiting for you."

"Yes, I'm making my way as quickly as possible. But, I'm calling to find out what happened. You didn't leave any details in your phone message."

"Father Cameron, it's all so sad. The Chief of Police just called me and told me everything." Father Cameron couldn't help but note that Sarah sounded very self-important as she referenced the police chief. He closed his eyes and prayed for the patience to be less disapproving of this woman, whom he didn't know other than by name.

"According to Chief Johnson, Father Mario showed up *at the scene*." Father Cameron grimaced as she emphasized the words. "And apparently he just went into some delirium. Passed out cold and got a concussion when he hit the ground."

Father Cameron thought he heard satisfaction in Sarah's voice. "So he just has a concussion?"

"Yes, apparently so. I think they'll let him go later today – certainly by tomorrow."

"Thanks, Sarah, I appreciate the information. Like I said, I'm on my way." They said polite goodbyes as Father Cameron got into his car and backed out of the driveway. Pulling away from the house, he saw Margaret, the housekeeper, in the side yard tugging at weeds.

He thought again about Bishop Grogan and why the Bishop was so keen to drive in from Richmond. In spite of the mournful occasion, Father Cameron thought it would be a good time to invite the Bishop to dinner. He made a mental note to call Margaret to let her know a guest might be joining them this evening.

Father Cameron guessed the Bishop wouldn't be staying for long; that he'd probably just come up to help calm Father Mario's concerns and to offer assistance with the services. He knew that Bishop Grogan and Father Mario had known each other for many years and that the Bishop was a mentor to him. That must have been why Bishop Grogan was here.

Still, Father Cameron was prepared to offer the Bishop a room, should he wish to stay. It would be a good opportunity to strengthen their relationship. They could discuss theology and debate ongoing challenges in the post-Vatican II era, in lieu of the Vatican Council's attempt to bridge some of the chasms between the old Church and the modern world.

Yes, this was a tragic occasion to be sure. But good *could* come of it, Father Cameron felt certain.

CHAPTER FOURTEEN

Bishop Grogan stepped off the elevator and scanned the walls for directional signs. A nurse hurrying past asked over her shoulder, "Need help, Father?"

"523?"

"This way," she pointed as she continued along. "On the right."

Bishop Grogan mumbled his thanks but the nurse, who had never slowed her pace, had hurried off in another direction. He scanned the numbers on the doors as he passed until he found 523. The door was slightly ajar and he tapped it a couple of times as he pushed it open and stepped into the room.

His eyes first saw Sergeant Walker, whose chair was in the far corner, and then he saw Chief Johnson staring out the window. Momentarily startled, the Bishop thought he'd entered the wrong room. Then he saw Father Mario sleeping in the bed.

As the Bishop entered, Sergeant Walker stood and the Chief turned slowly around to meet the Bishop's curious stare.

"I'm Bishop Grogan from the Richmond Diocese. Thank you so much for looking after Father Mario until I could get here."

Sergeant Walker stepped forward, offered his hand, and introduced himself. Chief Johnson waited for the Bishop to reach out to him first – which he did immediately upon releasing Sergeant Walker's hand. The Bishop's surprise in learning that Father Mario had been under the careful supervision of the police chief didn't escape the two officers. At this point, every movement, every word, every expression would be observed, recorded, recalled, discussed and analyzed in the greatest of detail once they returned to the station.

"So, how is he?" the Bishop inquired after introductions, his voice assuming the whispered tones reserved for hospitals and funeral homes.

"He'll be all right in a few days," the Chief responded. "He got a concussion in his fall – unfortunate landing considering the grassy padding. The biggest concern at the moment is his state of emotional distress."

"Yes," the Bishop responded. "I heard the tragic news. Any idea on who could have done this heinous crime?"

"Not yet. It's still early."

The three men looked at each other. Finally the Bishop turned his gaze to Father Mario. He was wondering how much he would have to tell the police – if anything at all.

"I had a chance to speak to Sarah Pulley today," Chief Johnson said, deciding to get right down to business.

Bishop Grogan looked at the Chief and waited for him to go on. The name Sarah Pulley didn't ring any bells.

"Sarah, from St. Joseph's," the Chief added, waiting for a response.

"Oh, was she answering phones in the parish office today?"

the Bishop asked, damning himself that he didn't ask the name of the woman he talked to this morning and damning himself even more so that he didn't tell her to go home. Pulley, Pulley, Pulley – that name was sounding more familiar to him now.

"I guess so – she answered the phone when I called. I do believe she was the one who talked to you earlier today."

Bishop Grogan nodded his head as if it was all coming back to him now. He wasn't sure where this conversation was going.

"She mentioned that a rather large percentage of the congregation at St. Joseph's was unhappy with Father Mario. Apparently they had some...*concerns*."

Bishop Grogan looked quickly back to Father Mario, fearing he might have heard Chief Johnson, even though his eyes were shut and he appeared to be sleeping.

"Don't worry," the Chief said, reading the Bishop's mind. "The juice in the IV put him to sleep. He needs the rest."

Bishop Grogan exhaled with relief and turned sharply to the Chief. "Their concerns are completely unfounded and I oppose any and all actions the complainants have recommended."

"Are you certain that Father Mario knew nothing about the increasing discomfort of his parishioners and their desire to remove him from the parish?"the Chief asked.

"I only know what I have been assured by those who signed the petition," Bishop Grogan said. "I can certainly confirm that I have said nothing of it to anyone; especially given that there is no evidence to suggest any validity in their *concerns*. Personally I considered it rubbish from the beginning, although I was obligated to conduct a private investigation, after which my beliefs were clearly confirmed."

"But, what if he did find out? What if one of the parishioners informed him?"

"If that occurred, it is unknown to me."

The two men considered each other, neither breaking the eye contact that had been maintained during their curt exchange. In the corner, Sergeant Walker had quietly resumed his seat and was scribbling diligently. He looked up to observe the Bishop's demeanor and search for any signs of facial twitches, clenched hands, locked knees.

Chief Johnson resumed his questioning. "I understand that you believe Father Mario was unaware of the parishioners' petition to the Diocese regarding his removal. But, just for the sake of hypothesis, let's say he *had* known. Is it not worrisome to you that the family lying in the morgue – well, Mr. Conner to be exact – initiated the complaint and lobbied other parishioners to sign?"

"Chief Johnson, I am not in the business of hypothesizing about such things; that would be your job I do believe. As I stated, I do not see any credence in the petition. However, to be very clear, you could never convince me that Father Mario would be guilty of the accusations that were made. Never!" Bishop Grogan crossed himself at the very thought.

Again, the two men digested the conversation without breaking eye contact. Sergeant Walker noted that Bishop Grogan did not attempt to hide his anger at the Chief's implied scenario. His eyes had narrowed and his hands, which he'd clasped in front of him, had clenched before he released them to cross himself.

Sergeant Walker continued to watch from his corner chair until finally the Bishop turned away and walked to Father Mario's bedside. Leaning over, he gently picked up the priest's hand and began whispering what sounded like a prayer. When he finished, he made the sign of the cross on the sleeping man's forehead.

"If there's nothing more officers, I will take over Father Mario's care. I'm most grateful for your show of concern," Bishop Grogan said, with a renewed sense of calm.

It was a dismissal to be sure; an invitation to vacate unless there was a legal reason to remain – which there wasn't. Chief Johnson dropped his gaze to the floor and considered what more there could be. Sergeant Walker sat quietly, anticipating the Chief's next move.

"Sarah mentioned that Father Mario was good friends with a Father Cameron – from St. Mark's, I think? She said he would be meeting you here. Would you mind if I asked him a few questions as well?" Chief Johnson asked, pressing the Bishop further.

The Bishop had forgotten that Father Cameron should have been here and was grateful that, for whatever reason, he had not yet arrived.

"Father Cameron knows nothing about the complaint against Father Mario."

"I understand. However, if they were good friends, might Father Cameron have information that might be able to confirm or deny the parishioners concerns?"

"I cannot speak for what Father Cameron may or may not know. Question him if you must, but my preference would be that the complaints against Father Mario not become the headlines of tomorrow's papers."

Chief Johnson almost chuckled out loud. He had led the Bishop right where he wanted him and it had been so easy it was almost embarrassing.

"Bishop Grogan, you have a lot at stake here, don't you? I mean, either way you look at it, you have a potential scandal on your hands."

The Bishop stiffened, realizing too late where the Chief was going with his line of questioning. *Not a problem*, he thought. *I didn't realize the man would offer me such a challenge.* He decided to sharpen his thinking and get out of the hole he had fallen into.

"Chief Johnson, I respect your concern and understand your need for questioning. You are, after all, just doing your job and I have no intention whatsoever of standing in your way. I pray to God that you are successful in uncovering the responsible party for this crime; after all, even Jesus advocates the appropriateness of justice in an unjust world. Having said that, please understand that the Church is always under harsh criticism from non-Catholics – most of them purported *Christians*. This criticism has been exacerbated, as I'm sure you are well aware, by recent scandals." He paused to cross himself again. "Of course I am hoping to avoid any unfounded media attention with regard to the Church, my diocese and Father Mario. My hope is that only the truth be shared, whatever that truth may be – not unsubstantiated allegations that will likely destroy a good man's career."

The Chief nodded, respectfully. "I understand. Just one clarification if you don't mind: are you referring to possibly destroying Father Mario's career or was that comment regarding your own career?"

"You can draw your own conclusions, Chief Johnson," Bishop Grogan retorted through clenched teeth. "You seem to be quite astute at doing so already. Any further questions will need to be in the presence of Church counsel. And, that goes for Father Cameron as well."

"Don't you think he needs to be the one to make that call?"

"I've just made it for him."

As if on cue, a series of light raps were heard on the door and Father Cameron stepped into the room.

CHAPTER FIFTEEN

When he stepped into Father Mario's room, Father Cameron found himself looking into two faces he'd not seen before. Standing next to the bed was a red-faced Bishop Grogan.

"Hello, Father Cameron, I'm glad you could come. Police Chief Johnson and Sergeant Walker were just leaving," Bishop Grogan said, fanning his arm gracefully toward the door.

"Father," Chief Johnson nodded, as he walked past with Sergeant Walker right behind.

Father Cameron stood speechless, nodding in return as they left the room. He glanced over to the Bishop who signaled for him to close the door. He watched as the Bishop eased himself into the chair nearest Father Mario's bed and leaned forward to rest his head in his prayerful hands. The Bishop's thumbs were hooked underneath his chin, giving the natural low-hanging folds of skin an almost taut appearance. In that moment of illusion, Father Cameron could see why people desired cosmetic surgery. The Bishop's posture had taken years off of his face.

Father Cameron picked up the chair from the corner of the

room and brought it over to where the Bishop sat, head still resting in his hands. He sat and looked from the Bishop to Father Mario's sleeping face. In his mind he wrestled with whether or not to speak, but since his patience was lacking today he chanced opening the conversation.

"Bishop Grogan, is everything okay?"

The Bishop sighed deeply as he raised his head and looked at Father Cameron. "All is well, Father, all is well. I was just thinking about the ripple effect."

"The ripple effect..."

"Yes, you know how one little thing can touch something else, which touches something else and so on. Like a falling line of dominoes."

"Or, like the game *Pass It On* where one person shows an act to kindness to someone else who then passes that act of kindness on."

"Yes," the Bishop answered, realizing that Father Cameron's analogy was much more positive than his own. Undoubtedly, there was a difference between knocking down a line of dominoes that someone carefully lined up versus sharing random acts of kindness.

Father Cameron waited a moment before interrupting the silence.

"So, how's Father Mario? I understand that he suffered a concussion while at the Conners' house. What happened?"

The Bishop furrowed his brow. He was working hard to recall the part of the conversation regarding Father Mario's injury. "The police chief told me he got a concussion from a fall and was suffering from emotional distress. I didn't ask for details."

Father Cameron nodded, still wondering what had happened to Father Mario after their morning call and how he had ended up in the hospital with a concussion. And, if that wasn't enough, Father Cameron was more than surprised to walk in to find the Chief of Police in the room, in addition to the fact that the Bishop himself had made a special trip from Richmond.

"He looks out of it. Do you know when he'll be released?"

"No, I had only been here a few minutes before you arrived," Bishop Grogan responded wearily. "I haven't had the chance to talk to any of the nursing staff and I don't suppose the doctor will be around until later today."

Father Cameron couldn't help but notice how the folds of skin under the Bishop's chin now drooped down, hiding most of his neck, and making the Bishop once more the aged man that he was.

"Shall I go down and grab us some coffee?" Father Cameron was feeling a growing sense of concern for Bishop Grogan and decided his chances of spending time with the Bishop that evening would be greater if the Bishop were in higher spirits. "I can stop by the nurses' station on the way and see what I can learn."

"Not a bad idea, Father. I think I could use a cup of coffee right about now," the Bishop agreed. "As for Father Mario going home, my guess is that we'll have to wait for the doctor's evening rounds before we know more about that. In the meantime, I've brought paperwork that I need to catch up on."

"Yes, Excellency," Father Cameron replied, thinking that the Bishop's last comment about paperwork was a subtle message that he did not want to be disturbed with idle chat, much less theological debate. *That's okay*, Father Cameron thought. He knew there was still a possibility of dinner tonight, especially if it was after evening rounds before they knew whether Father Mario would be released. He reminded himself that he needed to call Margaret as he stepped into the hallway. His eyes scanned the hall for the nurses' station. To his right about twenty feet from the door stood the men in uniform who had just left. They seemed to be in conference with the nursing staff.

Chief Johnson spotted him right away and in the moment that Father Cameron paused to decide what to do first – go to the nurses' station or go downstairs for coffee – Chief Johnson had already begun walking in his direction. In what felt to Father Cameron an awkward moment, he found himself walking to meet the Chief. After all, he had a few questions, too.

CHAPTER SIXTEEN

"Father Cameron, I'm glad to have a chance to speak to you." Chief Johnson said, as he extended his hand to Father Cameron, a formality that had been ignored just moments earlier in Father Mario's room.

"Chief Johnson, Sergeant Walker." Father Cameron acknowledged both with a handshake and concerned expression. "I was just on my way to the nurses' station to see if I could learn a bit more about Father Mario's condition. All I know at the moment is that he has a concussion. I would like to have a better understanding of the circumstances surrounding this incident all together, if I could be frank."

Chief Johnson liked Father Cameron already. He was a man that didn't waste time getting to the point. "I could tell you what I know but you would probably want to hear it from the staff."

"Actually, I'd like to know what happened after he arrived at the Conners' home. I talked to him first thing this morning, just after he'd read the paper. As you know, he was taking the news really hard."

"Well, I can certainly fill you in on that part," Chief Johnson offered. "Father Mario was emotionally distressed when he arrived at the Conners' home and he passed out on the front lawn. When he fell, he hit his head and suffered a concussion."

Father Cameron nodded, not quite satisfied with Chief Johnson's answer. "Was there anything in particular that created additional emotional distress or was this just a result of...?" Father Cameron watched the Chief shift his weight. "How about we go down and grab some coffee? Do you have time to sit for a few minutes?"

Chief Johnson was in heaven. He wasn't asking Father Cameron to talk to him; rather, Father Cameron was inviting the conversation. Not that Chief Johnson worried about the Bishop's request for counsel; but, out of respect for the Church, he felt better that Father Cameron was leading and he was simply following. "Absolutely, coffee would be great," he quickly responded.

On the elevator ride down, Father Cameron elaborated on his morning call with Father Mario – minus the reference to the file in his top drawer. Father Cameron couldn't imagine losing an entire family from his congregation – it was too tragic even to consider. He chatted about meeting Father Mario in seminary and how intense he was as a theologian. He explained that he had been at St. Mark's for eight years and Father Mario at St. Joseph's for five.

The conversation made for nice filler – and they all knew that's what it was. Still, Chief Johnson and Sergeant Walker listened attentively.

In the hospital cafeteria, they stood in a short line for coffee,

Father Cameron getting an extra cup for the Bishop. When the men settled at a corner table offering a bit of privacy, Father Cameron directed his next set of questions to the Chief.

"I understand that Father Mario passed out after he got to the scene. What exactly happened? It's just not making sense to me."

"I guess Sergeant Walker could answer better than I, since he was standing next to Father Mario. I was in the house at the time."

Sergeant Walker cleared his throat, giving himself a minute more to collect his thoughts, and then he met Father Cameron's stare straight on.

"As best as I can determine," Sergeant Walker began, "Father Mario came to the Conner home to confirm what he'd read in the paper. He appeared quite shaken. I'm sure you understand that it is standard operating procedure for us to ask questions of neighbors, acquaintances, family and friends in hopes of finding anything that may help us piece together what might have happened. When I told Father Mario that Chief Johnson wanted to speak to him, he didn't respond. The next thing I knew he was on the ground. It all happened rather fast."

Father Cameron listened intently as Sergeant Walker spoke, trying to imagine the scene in his head. He visualized Father Mario driving to the Conner home, confirming his worse fears, speaking to the officers and then suddenly dropping to the ground. Since Father Cameron had talked to Father Mario right after he'd read the morning paper, he knew how much pain Father Mario was in. "And then what?"

This time Sergeant Walker looked over to the Chief and Father Cameron's eyes followed, waiting for the story to continue.

"We called for an ambulance and here we are," Chief

Johnson said, shrugging his shoulders. He waited to see what Father Cameron might share before saying more.

Father Cameron remained quiet and nodded his head slowly as he digested the information. Something still seemed oddly out of place and he considered for a moment what that might be. He watched the Chief take a sip of his coffee, set the cup down on the table and begin to spin the cup slowly in place. "So, how is it that you came to be here? Are you waiting for him to regain consciousness so you can question him?"

Chief Johnson realized that Father Cameron was trying to understand Father Mario's actions just as they were. At this point, the Chief understood that Father Cameron was not likely to offer up anything without being prompted first. This meant that he would have to weigh angering the Bishop further if he took a chance with Father Cameron. Sensing that Father Cameron's communication style was systematic and analytical, the Chief chose his words carefully.

"No, we don't plan to question him today, but most probably in the next couple of days. It will be important to learn as much as we can about the Conner family and I expect Father Mario will be able to provide a very important glimpse into their lives."

"It would be good if you could wait until after the funeral and the shock of it all has had time to pass," Father Cameron said. "In the meantime, I understand from Father Mario that the family was very active in the Church, so I'm sure you could talk to some of the parishioners if you needed more detail right away."

Father Cameron's last words confirmed for Chief Johnson what the Bishop had said earlier – he had no knowledge of the parishioners' complaint against Father Mario. Unless, of course,

Father Cameron was trying to tell them something. Maybe they weren't the good friends he had been led to believe.

"Was Father Mario happy in his parish? Did he get along well with the parishioners?"

Father Cameron looked at the Chief and furrowed his brow. "I'm not sure what kind of question that is Chief Johnson, but what I can say is that Father Mario is very happy. He cares deeply for his parish, the families and the Catholic Church. You may not know that he is a Protestant convert – and any cradle Catholic will tell you that those who choose Catholicism are almost excessive in their dedication. I can assure you, there is not a more devoted priest, and I'm convinced that his parishioners recognize and admire him for that fact."

"The fact that he was a convert?" the Chief asked, testing Father Cameron's sense of humor.

"The fact of his absolute devotion to his parish and the Church," Father Cameron answered emphatically, missing the Chief's joke.

"Exactly how does one measure absolute devotion?" Chief Johnson asked.

Father Cameron studied Chief Johnson, not sure if the question was making fun or a legitimate inquiry. Since Father Cameron had been praying for patience all day, he decided to give the police chief the benefit of the doubt.

"There is no exact form of measurement – it is subjective, of course. In this case, the observations are my own. I have known Father Mario since seminary and consider him a personal friend. His conversion to the Catholic Church and attending the seminary were life-changing events for him, which he frequently talks about in our discussions."

"I didn't realize conversion was such a big deal."

"Then you must not be Catholic."

"Not yet, but I might be by the time I uncover any leads to why a husband, wife and three innocent children were murdered early this morning as they slept."

Chief Johnson left those words to digest as the men sat looking at each other. This time it was Father Cameron who broke the gaze as he sipped his coffee. His eyes remained lowered as he set his cup down. In his mind, he was hearing Father Mario's voice this morning, cracking with the pain of emotion, *Rick, you know what this could have been...* But, he couldn't mention that to Chief Johnson, the Bishop forbade it. Father Cameron wondered if that might be considered obstruction of justice. Yes, probably so. He would be forced to bring it up to the Bishop, perhaps over dinner. As remote as it might be, he was certain the police would want to know about it, especially now.

The Chief sat patiently. He could see that his words had triggered deep thought for Father Cameron, just as he hoped they would. Whether or not Father Cameron opened up, Chief Johnson could only guess. His guess was leaning toward not.

"I'd best get this coffee up to the Bishop. Thanks for answering my questions. I shall pray daily that you find resolution in this case." Father Cameron rose slowly and extended his hand graciously across the table toward the Chief, who had risen, along with Sergeant Walker.

"Father Cameron, one last thing," Chief Johnson began, as he released the priest's hand. "I rode with Father Mario in the ambulance on the way to the hospital. He was in and out of consciousness so his state of mind may not have been completely lucid. However, he did mention something about threats against the Church and Bishop Grogan's unwillingness to acknowledge any possible danger. Are you aware of what Father Mario was referring to?"

Father Cameron was both relieved and frightened. The Bishop had been so adamant about not speaking further on the subject, just hearing Chief Johnson speak of it to him made his heart race. Still, he felt comforted in some way. The word was out, sort of, and now they would all have to speak to it.

"I am aware," was all he said as he picked up the two cups from the table and turned to go, leaving the Chief and Sergeant starring after him.

CHAPTER SEVENTEEN

Chief Johnson and Sergeant Walker walked out of the hospital and into the hot July sun. They made their way slowly across the parking lot to the patrol car as the heat waves danced off the black asphalt. Sergeant Walker waited at the passenger's door while the Chief searched his pockets for the keys. Remembering that he had driven the Chief's car to the hospital, Sergeant Walker reached into his pocket to pull them out and toss them over the car to the Chief's hand.

Neither man said anything as they got into the sweltering car. Chief Johnson started the engine and immediately rolled down all the windows. The blistering heat rising from the asphalt was less oppressive than the air that had been trapped inside the car. His mind flashed back to the early morning hours and how wonderful the air had felt coming in through the windows. *Too bad I was on my way to a murder scene.*

Just as Chief Johnson put the car in reverse to pull out, his cell phone rang. He pulled it from his shirt pocket and looked at the number before answering.

"Chief Johnson."

There was a moment of silence while the Chief listened.

"Call me when you find the dog."

Chief Johnson disconnected the call and looked over at Sergeant Walker. "Apparently, the Conners had a dog. Did you see any sign of a dog?"

"No." Sergeant Walker replayed his numerous walk-throughs in his mind. "Was it an indoor or outdoor dog?"

"Indoor, according to neighbors."

"I don't even recall seeing a food or water bowl. And, when we looked through the kitchen pantry and cabinets, I have no recollection of seeing dog food."

"Typically, a dog would have stayed with its family, even if they were dead," Chief Johnson said, thinking out loud. "I have seen cases where a family pet might have wandered off, but in that case the dog was in a state of shock resulting from a gunshot wound. I've never seen or heard of a dog leaving the family home carrying its food bowl on its back."

Sergeant Walker continued to replay the crime scene in his mind and the Chief's attempted joke didn't even register. In spite of the Chief's humor and Sergeant Walker's deep concentration, both men were thinking of just one thing: who would have killed the entire family and then taken the dog?

"What kind of dog?" Sergeant Walker asked.

"Black cocker spaniel. Went by the name of Calvin."

"A cocker spaniel would have definitely been a shedder."

"Yep. Should have been dog hair all over the place."

"I didn't see any dog hair on the floor or furniture. Mrs. Conner must have been a manic cleaner. Maybe the forensics team picked some out of the carpet or off the sofa. I guess we'll have to wait to get the report."

"In the meantime, maybe we should put an APB out on the dog. You never know..."

Sergeant Walker looked over at the Chief to gauge his seriousness. With Chief Johnson, one could never really know.

"Think about it," the Chief said. "This is going to be a big story. It will go nationwide and maybe even be picked up in some international press. We can use the dog as a means to engage the public. Think about it, it's easier to save a dog than to turn a neighbor in as a possible murder suspect. Except in the case of Sarah Pulley..." Chief's voice trailed off and the two men sat in silence, each in his own world of thought.

Ten minutes later, the Chief was pulling into the parking lot of St. Joseph's. He looked over at Sergeant Walker and smiled. "Father Cameron did encourage us to talk to the parishioners. No need procrastinating."

CHAPTER EIGHTEEN

Sarah Pulley was on the phone all day, calling an emergency meeting of the committee that had formed with the sole purpose of ousting Father Mario. Most committee members had already read the news and were frightened and shocked beyond belief. Many, like Sarah, had wondered if word of their committee had leaked out and if the death of the Conner family – as unbelievable as it seemed – could somehow be linked to their controversial efforts.

Yes, there had been some controversy within the parish membership as not all members of the church believed, as did the affiliates of this special committee, that Father Mario was a bad man. In fact, there had been some heated debate among several church families on this very topic. Perhaps word had gotten out. But even so, who could have massacred an entire family? Who could have killed three innocent children?

In spite of their fears, most of the committee members arranged to meet at the church at 3:00 p.m. to discuss what steps should be taken next. Their appeal to the Bishop seemed to have gone nowhere, but now there was increasing reason to suspect that something was terribly wrong with Father Mario.

In the now permanent absence of Allen Conner, the initial complainant against Father Mario who had formed the committee and recruited its members, Sarah Pulley had taken charge. She greeted the members with great seriousness as they joined her in the parish meeting room.

All eyes were fixed on Sarah as she recalled the day's events, beginning with the call from the police station, then her personal discussion with the Bishop (now much elaborated) and finally her heart-to-heart with Police Chief Carl Johnson. Where many people would have lost their way in such tragedy and chaos, Sarah Pulley seemed to thrive on it. Drastic times called for drastic actions and she was in charge now. Having been only an administrator all of her adult life, she would now show she could be a leader. Yes, even under these circumstances, she would lead this committee to achieve its goal. It would be a tribute to the Conner family, she would make certain of it.

Just as she was closing her passionate ode to Allen Conner and family, the meeting room door opened and Chief Johnson stepped through, followed by Sergeant Walker. The assembly shifted uncomfortably and looked to Sarah for assurance.

"Officers, may I assist you?" Sarah asked, guardedly.

"Yes, I'm Police Chief Carl Johnson and this is Sergeant Walker. We were hoping to speak to Sarah Pulley."

"I'm Sarah Pulley, Chief Johnson, the one with whom you spoke earlier. Why don't we step into the church offices so we can speak privately?"

As they moved to the next room, the Chief made his request.

"Actually, I wanted to ask you for the names of other parishioners who we could talk to, but it looks like you've got a group here already. Do you mind if we speak to some of the families now?

Sarah stiffened. "I'm sorry, Chief Johnson, but when we spoke on the phone about my availability, I specifically told you I had a committee meeting and wouldn't be available to talk to you until 6:00 p.m. This is a private church meeting and everyone is still digesting the tragedy of losing one of our most active parish families. Perhaps I could give you a list of names tomorrow and you could contact them at a more convenient time?"

"I couldn't help but overhear some of your discussion," the Chief paused and considered Sarah for a minute. Her face reddened slightly but she maintained her stance. "It seems like the topic of your meeting is what brings us here. I'd like to have the chance to speak to folks sooner rather than later. I'm sure you can understand the urgency. It's quite a blessing that you pulled this meeting together, given the circumstances. If we could take just a little of your time, it would help us dig deeper into this terrible tragedy."

Chief Johnson watched Sarah's face soften as he acknowledged her understanding and importance in this desperate matter. She seemed to stand taller and she nodded her head as if in agreement with the Chief in his keen observations. Not to mention, the Chief's use of the word *blessing* always worked with self-proclaimed Christians – Protestant and Catholic alike. "How would you like to proceed?" she asked.

Chief Johnson considered for a moment the best way forward. He had done a quick count when he first stepped into the room. There were fifteen men and women in the meeting, including Sarah, and he wanted to speak to each of them separately. He also wanted to avoid the group talking among themselves while the interviews were being conducted.

Chief cleared his throat but then began speaking in a whisper, forcing both Sarah and Sergeant Walker to lean in to hear.

"I'll ask Sergeant Walker to talk to the group to help prepare them for the interviews, which I will conduct in the back corner of your meeting room, if it's okay."

"Of course," Sarah responded. "Shall we rejoin the group?"

When they returned to the meeting room only eight parishioners remained. Those who had stayed provided a variety of urgent needs to excuse the members who had quickly departed through the back door of the meeting room.

Chief Johnson looked at Sarah and asked in his most humble tone if she would be so kind as to explain why they were here and what the process would be for interviewing. He watched as she glowed with self-importance and assumed her leadership role within the remaining circle.

While Sarah spoke to her fellow parishioners, the Chief instructed Sergeant Walker to give those in wait a long-winded description of past investigations and legal procedures laced with police lingo – makes folks feel in the loop, he said. While Sergeant Walker entertained the crowd, Chief Johnson would set up by the back door and ensure that those interviewed exited the door and did not rejoin the group. He would start, of course, with Sarah Pulley.

Chief Johnson gave Sergeant Walker a pat on the shoulder, walked toward the back of the room, set up two chairs and smiled warmly at Sarah as he motioned for her to join him.

CHAPTER NINETEEN

Father Cameron made his way back to room 523, where his friend and brother in the Church lay resting peacefully. Sitting in the chair next to the bed keeping vigil was Bishop Grogan. His lap was strewn with papers and he held a pen in his hand, but his attention rested on Father Mario. Father Cameron placed the Bishop's coffee on the table parked at the foot of the bed and rolled it over to where the Bishop sat.

Bishop Grogan reached for the coffee, removed the lid and blew gently before taking a long sip. Father Cameron remembered that he'd put creamer and sugar in his pants pocket and he quickly retrieved them and placed them on the tabletop. The Bishop nodded his head in acknowledgment and paused to consider Father Cameron. His gaze made the priest shuffle uncomfortably and Father Cameron walked to the window and looked out into the hot afternoon.

"I'm not sure how long you plan to stay, Bishop Grogan," Father Cameron began. "But I would be most delighted for you to stay the evening in the parish home. Margaret is a splendid cook, and it's a shame that only I enjoy the benefits of our benefactor, Louisa Armstrong."

Bishop Grogan inhaled deeply. Instead of responding to Father Cameron's offer, he began to tell him stories of his youth, of growing up in upstate New York, of his hard-working parents, of his mediocrity as a student and of his only brother.

Father Cameron didn't know why the Bishop, who was known to be a very private and closed man, had chosen him, or this particular time, to share the intimacies of his life. He believed that most men of the cloth were led to the priesthood by some significant event or series of events in their lives; that was certainly true for him. He also knew it to be true of Father Mario, but he had never learned Bishop Grogan's story. That deeply personal part of his life had never been revealed. As Father Cameron listened to the Bishop, he sensed melancholy – a sad longing for years passed.

Bishop Grogan stopped his autobiography only when a nurse came in to check on Father Mario. He took that opportunity to ask the nurse about Father Mario's possible release and confirmed that he could leave today once the doctor came by and signed the release form. They watched as she checked the IV, which had long ago dripped the last of its clear fluid into the tubing connected to Father Mario's arm.

The nurse stood over the sleeping man and called his name loudly until the slumbering priest turned his face to her and slowly opened his eyes.

"Stephen Mario?" the nurse called again.

"Yes," he answered hoarsely.

"Stephen, you've had a nice, long nap. Are you feeling better now?" she asked.

"Yes, much better," he echoed. "Can I go back to sleep now?"

"No, you need to stay awake. Dinner will be here soon and the doctor will be making rounds. Besides, you have company," she said, as she turned on her heel and left the room.

With the nurse out of his line of vision, Father Mario turned his head to see Father Cameron standing next to the window. Father Cameron nodded supportively and then motioned toward the Bishop. When Father Mario turned to see Bishop Grogan seated next to his bed, his eyes teared. Bishop Grogan stood to console him and assure him that all was well. Father Cameron stood quietly watching.

CHAPTER TWENTY

It didn't take long for Chief Johnson to go through the interviews. His questions were standard and open-ended: What can you tell me about the Conner family? Do you have any reason to believe that someone would want to harm them? Why are you affiliated with this committee, why do parishioners want to relieve Father Mario of his position at St. Joseph's?

For Sarah Pulley, he asked her for the names of those parishioners who had left after the Chief showed up to ask questions. He also wanted the names of every committee member who had advocated for Father Mario's removal.

Sarah was caught by surprise when, at the end of her interview Chief Johnson thanked her and ask her to exit the back door. Sensing her embarrassment at her dismissal, Chief Johnson confirmed that Sarah was key to their investigation. Looking over her shoulder at the circle of parishioners she was leaving behind, Sarah headed to the back door with some hesitation. Inside, no one even noticed her departure.

Just after Chief Johnson's last interview, an elderly priest came in through the door at the front. Surprised at seeing the two police officers, he jumped back for a moment before regaining his composure.

"Good evening, officers, I'm Father Patrick. I didn't realize there was a meeting ongoing and I was just coming in to turn off the light."

"Good evening, Father Patrick," the Chief answered as he and Sergeant Walker stood. "The timing is perfect as we were just leaving and I was wondering how to lock up."

"Lock up?" the old man answered with a chuckle. "Why, there was a time that church doors were always open. Now-a-days, everything must be under lock and key. No worries, you two, I'll take care of everything."

"I don't mean to sound rude," the Chief began, as the three men left the meeting room and headed toward the front door of the church, "but are you one of the priests here?"

"Oh no," Father Patrick responded. "Bishop Grogan called me and said that Father Mario was sick and would be out for a bit. I'm a traveling priest and go wherever I'm needed. I haven't been to St. Joseph's in years – not since the last priest was here – that would have been... why, his name escapes me. Anyway, a priest or two ago it was, and a bad case of pneumonia, kept me here for a good six weeks or so."

Chief listened as the priest rattled on in a cadence that was uniquely not American but interesting to hear. Once at the front door, the priest reached into a leather pouch he had been carrying and pulled out a large skeleton key that reminded Chief of some medieval relic. As they stepped outside the big heavy doors, Father Patrick took the key and inserted it into the aged bronze metal plate on the door. He turned the key and counted each click, click, click until satisfied. Then he slowly pulled the dark key from the cavernous lock and returned it to his leather pouch before straightening his old and frail body and turning to face the two men.

"Do you need a ride," Chief asked, not certain where the old man would be headed and noticing that the only car left in the parking lot was his own.

"Why no, I'm just walking around the bend here. There is a parish house right behind the church and that's as far as I need to go. I wish you gentlemen a good evening and hope to see you at noon Mass tomorrow." Father Patrick clapped one arm around the Chief's shoulders and the other around Sergeant Walker while ushering them down the stairs. Chief Johnson wasn't sure if he was given them a polite dismissal or using them to help himself down the three steps to the sidewalk.

The Chief made a friendly wave as they watched Father Patrick disappear around the corner of the church. It wasn't even 5:00 p.m., and the day was still hot and bright.

"What say ye join me for a bowl of stew and arsh taters," Chief asked in a mock brogue. "I'm sure me old lady will have something nice fixed up for us."

"Thanks, Chief," Sergeant Walker answered with a slight smile. "I think I'll go back to the station and see if forensics has black dog hair. I'll go through my notes and talk to Lacey to see what leads he may have."

"Don't forget to ask for Special Investigator Zach's opinion. He's going to be quite a detective one of these days. You could probably learn a thing or two from him."

"Yeah, right. I'll not forget about Zach." Sergeant Walker said, remembering the earlier deception when Zach had read his notes from over his shoulder and then used the information to answer Chief Johnson's question.

"I'll drop you off at the station, but I won't be staying. I need to take care of some other business," Chief said, his mind already on his next steps. "Let everyone know that at 0700 they need to be here, bright-eyed and bushy tailed. We'll see what we've got and what we need to do next. I want everyone ready to give me something."

"Yes, sir. Can do."

"Oh, and call the local animal shelters, pounds, etc. See if anyone has a black cocker. If we can't find him in the next 24 hours, he'll become the lead story. We'll need to look through the family photos to see if we can get a good one of the dog."

"Yes, sir."

"Aren't you going to write that in your little notebook, along with all those other pages of notes you have?" the Chief asked, poking fun of the always serious sergeant.

"I can't read or write while I'm riding in a car. Makes me sick." Sergeant Walker kept his gaze steady out the front window.

"You always this intense?"

Sergeant Walker turned to look at the Chief, the man who had been the rock of the Hampton police force for the last 12 years. Chief Johnson was known for being hands on – he liked being in the mix and often took the lead on cases, even though his investigators wished he'd keep to his office. Sergeant Walker had only been on the force for two years, and the last couple of months he'd been lucky enough to shadow the Chief on a couple of big cases. He'd been taking a lot of heat from the guys at the station too and had been branded as "DB," short for Daddy's Boy.

Whether or not the Chief knew of the harassment he'd endured as a result of Chief Johnson's interest in him, Sergeant Walker didn't know. It didn't really matter anyway. What was important was that the Chief seemed to understand him and how he could intuitively read a person. Chief Johnson was like that too, it seemed. *If only everyone could tune into their internal natures and hear the voice within – warning, encouraging, calling,* he thought.

"Yes," he finally responded. "I guess I am."

CHAPTER TWENTY-ONE

Father Stephen Mario was stuck in a never-ending dream, a repeat of his childhood. He was five and his father found him playing house in the back yard with two neighbor girls – he was lovingly holding a bottle up to one of the four dolls – while the girls swept the grass with straw brooms. Livid that his son was playing like a girl, he jerked him up by the arm and dragged him into the house where he held the young boy in front of his mother's face while he ranted about her making such a pussy out of his son.

His father's frequent emotional outbursts left his mother a shrinking violet, and gave the young boy all the more reason to retreat into his own fantasyland. This seemed to further enrage his truck-driving father, who would leave for weeks at a time without coming home.

Stephen Mario's mother had been the part-time church administrator at the First Assembly of God, for as long as he could remember. She never reproached her husband nor inquired to his whereabouts. When money would get tight, she would pinch pennies and ask for cleaning work wherever she could find it. Somehow they always seemed to get through until the next time his father would show up expecting a hot meal and a clean house.

Then his dreamed changed and he was getting ready for his first day of school. His mother was beaming with excitement as she helped him dress. She took his hand and led him to the bathroom where she filled a cup with warm water and dipped a comb to slick back his hair. But when his father walked in and saw his son smiling proudly at himself in the mirror, everything changed. For reasons that, to this day, Father Mario couldn't understand, his father barreled into the bathroom and batted his mother's arm so hard that the comb went flying out of her hand and bounced off the wall into the toilet bowl. He remembers watching the small, black comb float back to the top after its plunging dive.

His mother at first looked shocked and frightened, but then he saw her eyes darken with a silent rage. His father must have seen it too, for he turned to leave but not before yelling that no wife of his would make a sissy-assed faggot out of his son.

That was Stephen Mario's last memory of his father, for when he left on his next road trip he never returned home. Neither son nor mother ever spoke of him, but Stephen remained secretly fearful that any day his father would show up and throw their peaceful, quiet world into a state of chaos. This fear kept him ever vigilant and, even in his dream, a chill ran down his spine.

This was followed by a series of dreams where Michael Conner, the older of the Conner sons, and Kevin Larson, the son of another parish member, were chasing after him throwing stones. Suddenly he was in his boyhood neighborhood and his mother was standing in the door of their house calling him to come in from play. Throughout the series of dreams, which seemed to repeat without end, Father Mario could hear a deep, soothing voice telling him that he would be okay.

When he awoke to find Father Cameron and Bishop Grogan there, he was both relieved and frightened. It was all coming back to him now, the morning news, driving to the Conners' home, being asked to speak with the police chief.

A wave of nausea overwhelmed him and he began to retch. Father Cameron raced around the bed to grab the pink plastic bedpan from the side table and held it up to Father Mario as he leaned dangerously over the side of the bed. Bishop Grogan put his hand on Father Mario's head and gave it a gentle pat. "Don't worry son, everything is in God's hands."

Dinner arrived and was immediately sent back out without even a glimpse of the offering. The smell of food had sent Father Mario into another retching fit, and Bishop Grogan was fearful that if they couldn't calm him down, the doctor would refuse to release him. Fortunately, by the time the doctor arrived shortly after 6:00 p.m., Father Mario was resting quietly. The doctor woke him, checked his record, asked a few questions and then signed his release forms.

When Father Mario stepped into the bathroom to change out of the hospital gown and back into his clothes, Bishop Grogan accepted Father Cameron's offer to spend the evening at the Armstrong home. He also told Father Cameron that he thought it best for Father Mario to spend a few days there as well. Without saying so directly, the Bishop wanted to ensure

Father Mario was supervised.

As the three men walked toward the elevator, Bishop Grogan suddenly stopped. "Father Mario, I'm afraid you must have left your collar back in the room."

Father Mario reached up to where his collar should have been and faced the Bishop in a moment of uncertainty.

"I was so distraught this morning over the news that I left home without it. My deepest apologies."

Bishop Grogan patted Father Mario on the back sympathetically. "Not to worry son, I've done that once or twice myself. Let's go then."

CHAPTER TWENTY-TWO

Chief Johnson pulled away from the station after dropping off Sergeant Walker – he had no plans to go back into the office today. He needed some space and wished that instead of his patrol car he could be driving Darlene, his 1971 Nova SS that he'd restored himself. Her body was in perfect condition and painted torch red. He had her riding on rally wheels with BF Goodrich raised white-letter tires. She turned heads wherever they went. Today would be a good day for an evening drive – maybe he and his wife Tanya would take Darlene for a drive to the beach.

He pulled out his phone to call Tanya. She'd just be getting off work and instead of her going home and wondering what to cook for dinner, he'd suggest they go out. Steamed crabs were sounding really good. Then he remembered he had one other call to make first.

The Chief pulled the car over on the side of the road and began scrolling through his contact list for the number of Julia Frank, the savvy reporter who had picked up last night's call over the police band to the Conners' residence. Julia had been there within minutes of the police and before the Chief's own arrival – didn't that woman ever sleep? He pressed the talk button after pulling up her number and Julia picked up on the second ring.

"Julia Frank, my favorite investigative reporter – who, by the way, never sleeps!"

Julia recognized the Chief's voice immediately – just the voice she wanted to hear.

"Chief Johnson, you know the media has been waiting all day for you to make a statement about the Conner murders. C'mon, what's the holdup? Not got anything to go on?" Julia knew she could chide the Chief – they had a good relationship. They were both well-known and respected – and considered role models in their African American community.

"Julia, Julia -- didn't Lacey tell you I'd be making a statement first thing in the morning? You know it's still early and we don't want to make any premature statements." Chief Johnson was using his deepest, smoothest voice. He had known it to be effective in many ways, especially with the lady-folk.

"Well, can you tell me who was whisked away in the ambulance this morning?"

"Jesus, were you still there?"

"No way. I sent my cracker-ass intern."

"Now Julia, you know that language is not politically correct."

"It's correct," she shot back. "He's the privileged, white-assed, snot-nosed kid of Congressman Wallace – need I say more? The kid talked daddy into sending him to the UNC School of Journalism and Mass Communication. It's supposedly one of the best journalism schools in the country, but let me tell you – that boy couldn't shoot a printable photo if I held the camera and

93

all he had to do was press the shutter."

"Julia, so much anger. You know, we have a black president now, you can let it all go." The Chief knew that Julia had come up the hard way, just like he had. He knew how hard it was to let go of the past. Still, he tried to ease the situation, just as he always did.

"Yeah, we'll see how much things change. I remain skeptical. After all, he's half white."

"Girl, you got issues. Let's talk about something that will make you happy."

Julia took a deep sigh. "What 'cha got for me?"

"Not for public consumption yet. Got it?"

"Yes, Chief, of course. Now hit me."

"Whoever murdered the Conner family may have taken the family dog, a black cocker spaniel with white on its chest. Named Calvin."

"You got to be kidding me. Is this some kind of joke? Am I supposed to get excited about a dog named Calvin?"

"Julia, *think* about it. Family murdered, dog missing. If we can find the dog, we could have a damn good lead on the killer."

"So, you don't have a lead, do you?" When the Chief didn't respond Julia shifted her thinking to how the dog angle could work. "What if the dog just ran away? I mean, that would be a pretty scary thing to witness, even for a dog."

"Then he'll get picked up. But, the dog was an indoor dog and when we went through the house there were no signs of a dog. No hair balls rolling across the floor, no food or water bowls – nada, nothing."

Julia was quiet. "How long until we can print some real news?" She was an investigative journalist, not some feature goo-

goo writing stories about lost dogs. No Marley for her, thank you very much.

"If we can't locate the dog tomorrow then we're going to go all out on the dog story. You'll have it first – you know, gotta keep it in the family."

"Uh-huh. Yeah, let me think about this one. So, are you gonna tell me who was whisked away in the ambulance?"

"See you tomorrow, Julia. Gotta run for now."

As Julia was about to ask her next question, the line went dead. She hated it when anyone cut her off like that. She muttered an obscenity under her breath and looked for Detective George Lacey's number. She knew that the Chief hated making media statements, and he had trained his officers to hold the press off as long as possible.

Chief Johnson eased the patrol car back onto 64 toward home, feeling satisfied with his call to Julia. He knew she was already writing the story in her head, in spite of her protest. He also knew that she'd have every one of her contacts looking for a little black cocker spaniel named Calvin without any of them even knowing why. Julia was good people. Smart, relentless and damn good at what she did – his kind of folk.

Instead of calling Tanya, Chief Johnson decided he'd try to beat her home. He'd get in, make her an apple martini, put on Albert King's *I'll Play the Blues for You* and greet her at the door with flowing compliments on how good she was looking.

He'd then suggest that she take a break from cooking and let him take his two favorite women out for steamed crabs. Although Darlene never seemed jealous of Tanya, the Chief believed that every once in a while Tanya would like to slash Darlene's tires.

He smiled at the thought, turned on his lights and pressed the gas. They were gonna have some good lovin' going down tonight.

CHAPTER TWENTY-THREE

Bishop Grogan insisted on driving Father Mario back to the Armstrong home, which gave Father Cameron the chance to call Margaret to let her know that guests would be coming for dinner. She indicated no alarm with this news; if anything, he thought she sounded pleased. *She must get so bored of just seeing me,* he thought.

When they arrived, Margaret was at the door with a formal welcome. She remembered, with some distaste, Bishop Grogan – whom she had overheard make boorish remarks about Louisa, her faithful employer for so many years. Louisa had ensured Margaret's continued service at the home in her will, which stated that Margaret would stay on at the Armstrong house after the transfer to Church assets.

There was some discussion about the appropriateness of having a woman living in a house with a priest. Ultimately, the Church made an exception and accepted the gift with gratitude. This is why, of course, that Father Cameron was the only priest who lived in such a lavish home, with his own female live-in maid/cook/gardener/errand-runner.

Margaret also knew Father Mario, who was a frequent visitor and dinner guest. Father Mario loved Margaret's mashed potatoes best of all and she always prepared them when she knew he would be coming for dinner. One look at Father Mario was all it took for Margaret to guess that something was terribly wrong. His tall figure was frail and his normally cheery disposition was encased in a pale shell of distance and self-absorbed pain.

She quickly led the way to the dining room where three place settings were laid out. As the men took their seats, Bishop Grogan at the head, Margaret whisked into the kitchen and came back with a bowl in each hand. Two more trips to the kitchen and their food was on the table, water was poured and a bottle of Chianti Reserve sat on the table in front of them.

Bishop Grogan bowed his head to recite the dinner prayer. "Bless us, O Lord, and these gifts, which we are about to receive from Thy bounty, through Christ our Lord. Amen"

"Amen," echoed the two priests.

As Father Cameron poured the wine, Bishop Grogan launched into his marinated cucumber salad – one of Margaret's classic summer salads. Three breasts of chicken lay in a small bowl, covered in a simple sauce of chicken broth and lemon juice. The chicken piccata was accompanied with rice florentine, one of Father Cameron's favorites, as he was especially fond of the parmesan topping that Margaret artfully managed. The last small bowl consisted of sliced honeydew melon and mango.

While they ate, Bishop Grogan talked about the latest Church politics. How Church officials were hoping to meet with

President Obama to discuss rights of the unborn. How intimately one should probe into the religious and spiritual beliefs of hospice patients. Then there was the never-ending debate around contraception.

Throughout the Bishop's well-articulated monologue, the two priests sat quietly and listened, with the exception of Father Cameron's contribution on hospice care. Father Mario, on the other hand, ate minimally, listened respectfully and nodded intermittently while the Bishop pontificated.

When dinner came to its natural close, Bishop Grogan surprised them.

"It seems that the Conner tragedy requires me to disclose some information that will likely be shocking to you both. I'm quite sure that what I have to share will be very painful for you in particular, Father Mario." The Bishop then turned to Father Cameron and, handing over the keys to his car, asked him to retrieve the brief case from the backseat of his car.

Father Cameron took the keys and made his way to the front door where he exited into the still too-warm evening. He unlocked the Bishop's Cadillac DeVille and opened the back door where he saw the black leather portfolio that he had seen earlier in the day at the hospital. He picked it up and walked back into the house.

While Father Mario and the Bishop waited in silence, Father Mario's mind raced as he tried to discern what the Bishop could possibly be referencing. After a short moment the Bishop suggested that they leave the dining room and move to a more private area for discussion.

Bishop Grogan and Father Mario were standing in the foyer

when Father Cameron returned. "I was thinking we could have this discussion in your office," the Bishop suggested as Father Cameron handed over his brief case and keys.

"Yes, of course," Father Cameron responded, leading the men through double doors opposite the dining room and into his office. He quickly turned the two leather chairs to face each other and rolled his own chair from behind the desk out to join the other two. As the three men sat, Bishop Grogan placed his brief case on the desk and folded his hands into his lap. For a moment he closed his eyes and inhaled deeply.

When Bishop Grogan opened his eyes, he looked directly at Father Mario. He cleared his throat before he spoke, giving both men an additional indication that whatever he was about to say was not going to be easy for him.

"Father Mario, what I am going to tell you is very painful for me to share and will be even more painful for you to hear. I want to say up front that I have totally dismissed this allegation after an obligatory investigation. Absolutely no action will be taken against you or any member of the church involved in the complaint. The only reason I share it with you now is due to what has happened today. You will undoubtedly be questioned about this during the police investigation and I want you to hear it from me first."

Bishop Grogan then told them about a letter he received from a secretly formed special committee at St. Joseph's – a letter asking for Father Mario's dismissal, due to inappropriate affection with two of the parish youth. As Bishop Grogan spoke those last words, a look of deep pain crossed Father Mario's face. His eyes slowly closed and he took a slow, deep breath. He began to shake his head from side to side as he dropped his chin to his chest.

Father Cameron sat in disbelief. He looked from Father Mario to the Bishop and back again. His heart was breaking, for he knew now that everything was about to change. Even if Father Mario were innocent of the accusation, if the media got wind of this – and likely they would – then Father Mario would be fighting an uphill battle. Scandal would ensue and the diocese would be in an upheaval. In every allegation of this nature, the effects were catastrophic.

Bishop Grogan reached for the briefcase and placed it in his lap. He clicked the brass clasps and opened the case just enough to retrieve a single sheet of paper. Then, closing the top gently, he clicked the brass clasps into their locks and placed the briefcase back onto the desk.

"I need to read you the letter. Then we will discuss the claims."

Father Mario was still shaking his head and his eyes remained closed even as he spoke. "Bishop Grogan, I can't do this. I can't do this now."

"I'm sorry Father Mario. Maybe I should have come to you with this as soon as I received it. But as I told you, I saw no credence – it just wasn't believable. Under normal procedure I would have suspended you from public ministry while the investigation was ongoing.

"Instead, I went to the Diocesan Review Board and staked my reputation and my position on your innocence. I asked for permission to conduct a private investigation, after which I presented the members of the board with the results. We unanimously agreed to dismiss the complaint.

"I apologize for putting you in this position now, but the police will want to talk to you and they likely already know about this; and if they don't, they will soon. For this reason, it is important – necessary – that you know now and have adequate time to consider how you will respond."

"I know how I will respond," Father Mario shot back. His eyes were open now and he looked hard at the Bishop. "I will respond with the truth of my innocence and put my faith in Christ Jesus that the truth will be made known."

Bishop Grogan was taken aback by the sudden fierceness of Father Mario's outburst. Uncertain how to respond, he picked up the letter and read aloud.

Dear Bishop Grogan:

Great sadness accompanies this letter that is being sent to you by concerned members of St. Joseph's in Hampton, VA. We pray that you receive it with God's blessing of compassion and understanding for our concerns. We trust that you will take the action necessary to restore our faith in our parish and our Church.

As a result of an incident reported between Father Mario and two boys of our parish, a special committee was formed to review the complaint and decide best next steps. The boys, who shall remain anonymous, both reported to their parents that Father Mario made them uncomfortable with inappropriate embraces while they were in the vestry removing their vestments after having served as altar boys.

Father Mario is young and we understand that the tradition of celibacy must be difficult at times. In lieu of making this situation public and causing a great deal of embarrassment to all, the committee is recommending the immediate removal of Father Mario as pastor.

In great faith, we await your response.

Sincerely,

Allen Conner

Allen Conner (on behalf of the special committee)

Bishop Grogan finished the letter and held it out for Father Mario, who shook his head in response. "I don't need to see it."

"Under the circumstances, I need to understand everything I can about this situation. Can you give me a different perspective from the one I have just shared? Have you perhaps embraced these young men in a way that would have made them uncomfortable?"

Father Mario's expression was far away. His earlier ferocity seemed to have relaxed into a calm sense of sadness and acceptance. "I have warmly embraced many of my parishioners, young and old. I have never felt anyone pull away from me in discomfort, nor has anyone ever made mention that my embrace was uncomfortable or unwelcome."

Bishop took a moment to consider Father Mario before responding. "You are the priest, your parishioners look up to you. You are the representative of Christ; they may not feel comfortable asking you not to embrace them."

"What you are really asking me, Your Excellency, is whether or not I have a tendency to play with boys."

"I'm sure that will be one of the first questions the police ask you, so you might as well practice responding to it," the Bishop volleyed back. He experienced his first twinge of doubt. Was it possible that this man, whom he had staked his reputation on, might somehow be guilty? He was suddenly struck by the paradox in a quote he had read recently by Presbyterian minister Frank Crane: *You may be deceived if you trust too much, but you will live in torment if you don't trust enough.* Which was it for him – had he been deceived or would this become the beginning of his torment?

Father Mario was experiencing his own paradox. In seminary, they had discussed the issues of celibacy and the temptations of priesthood at great length. In the end, they had committed to the faith and trust in their oaths and their pledge to serve the Lord God and the Catholic Church; this left no place for doubt.

"Excellency, let me begin by..."

The Bishop quickly held up his hand to interrupt. "Son, would you like to make a confession?"

"Excellency!" Father Mario was beginning to feel exasperated. "Confession, for what? So you won't have to give any statements or, God-forbid, should this become a big scandal, have to testify and reveal anything incriminating? That's our whole dilemma now, is it not? This requirement of confidentiality for confessions that forbids the Church to betray a penitent in any way and under any circumstances!" Suddenly Father Mario realized he had raised his voice at the Bishop, and he dropped his head into his hands in a sign of retreat.

All three men fell into a silence, each contemplating the Seal of the Confessional, which bound any priest hearing a confession to absolute secrecy. No circumstance or law could relinquish a priest from the burden of silence; not even to spare a life even it if it meant his own – and certainly not to avoid destruction of one's reputation or that of the Church. Violation of the Seal of Confession led to automatic excommunication according to Canon Law.

Judging Father Mario's dilemma by the passion of his remarks, Bishop Grogan carefully chose his next words. "Is one of the penitents that you protect one of the Conner boys?" he asked slowly yet firmly.

Father Mario met the Bishop's eyes and responded with a sense of sadness. "Yes."

Again the men sat in silence, each contemplating the complexity of the situation. Finally, Father Cameron offered to show them to their respective rooms for the evening and was shocked for the second time this evening by Bishop Grogan's words.

"We must discuss the file from last summer. It seems to have come up again in a most unlikely way."

Father Cameron thought back to earlier in the day when Chief Johnson had asked about the file and his sense of both fear and relief. Father Mario, on the other hand, appeared far away and completely removed from the statement the Bishop had just made.

Once again the Bishop cleared his throat and told the two priests about the Chief's questioning earlier in the day. "I'm not exactly sure how this information became known by the Chief of Police, but the fact is that he seems to have some knowledge and therefore we must be forthcoming in sharing what we know.

When Father Mario heard the Bishop's remarks he had a

quick glimpse, more like a feeling, of something related to this but he couldn't get his head around it. Something seemed familiar, yet nothing that he could really recall. The Bishop's willingness to discuss this issue was coming a little late as far as Father Mario was concerned.

Father Mario felt himself becoming somewhat perplexed and increasingly weary. He simply didn't know how much longer he could bear to keep his head up. All he really wanted to do was climb under a clean, crisp sheet and go to sleep. *Couldn't this wait?*

"I'm not going to ask if either of you know how this information fell into the hands of the police chief," the Bishop said, looking directly at Father Mario. "All that is important is that we understand why the Church did not act upon it."

As Bishop Grogan spoke, he suddenly realized that it was he who was not following normal protocol – not in the case of the letter from the special committee nor the information that lay in the file contained in his briefcase. In another moment of doubt, he began to see clearly what Chief Johnson might have been referring to – his own reputation could be seriously at stake here. How much did Chief Johnson know?

"Are you asking us to make a statement on behalf of the Church?" Father Cameron asked, not certain what Bishop Grogan was asking of them.

The Bishop didn't respond. He was still caught up in his own revelation and was beginning to feel as if a spider had spun a web around him. In his mind he heard himself reciting, 'Yea, though I walk through the valley of the shadow of death, I will fear no evil: for thou art with me; thy rod and thy staff they comfort me...'

"Excellency?" Father Cameron's voice called twice before the Bishop heard him.

"Yes?"

"Do you wish us to make a statement on behalf of the Church concerning the threats that were received last summer?"

Bishop Grogan felt another stitch of fear and his heart continued its prayer, *The LORD is my light and my salvation; whom shall I fear? The LORD is the strength of my life; of whom shall I be afraid? When the wicked, even mine enemies and my foes, came upon me to eat up my flesh, they stumbled and fell. Though a host should encamp against me, my heart shall not fear: though war should rise against me, in this will I be confident.* Only when his prayer was finished did he respond.

"No, I don't expect you to make statements on behalf of the Church. I simply expect you to tell the truth."

CHAPTER TWENTY-FOUR

Father Richard William Cameron lay awake in his bed when he heard the click of a door opening and then quiet footsteps passing by his doorway and down the stairs. He looked over at his bedside table and checked the clock – 5:00 a.m. Thinking it might be Father Mario or Bishop Grogan looking for an early cup of coffee, he hastily jumped from his bed, dressed and headed downstairs. As he got to the bottom step he saw the headlights of Bishop Grogan's car pulling out of the drive.

Now fully awake, Father Cameron headed toward the back of the house and into the kitchen to make coffee. It would be another hour before Margaret got up and he was appreciative for the silence of the house. He could use this time to work through the jumble of thoughts wracking his brain.

First there was a family murdered and Father Mario's belief that it had something to do with the papers in his desk. Then there were the strange happenings after Father Mario went to the Conner home – his collapse and subsequent hospitalization. All this followed by Bishop Grogan's hasty trip in from Richmond;

the odd conversation between the Hampton Chief of Police and himself; Bishop Grogan's revelation last evening that members of St. Joseph's had petitioned to have Father Mario removed from the parish for the *unthinkable;* and finally, Bishop Grogan's indication that both he and Father Mario should speak their truth if and when questioned by the police.

These were the things he thought about as he made coffee. He was thankful that Margaret thought to grind the coffee the evening before and leave it next to the coffee pot. Her thoughtfulness ensured that an early riser would not worry about waking others if grinding beans for the morning brew. *Maybe she does this every morning,* Father Cameron thought, realizing that it was a rare morning when he heard the beans grinding in the pot. Yet, the aroma of coffee greeted him with every waking day.

Order! he commanded his mind when all the happenings of the last day fought for his attention. *One thing at a time... it doesn't make sense now, but I've got to pray through this. God will give me the answers I need.* He crossed himself at the close of his silent prayer and watched the coffee drip into the pot.

Impatient for his first cup he walked over and removed the pot and placed his cup on the burner underneath the stream of fresh brew. When his cup was half-full, he switched it out with the coffee pot and raised the steaming cup to inhale its aroma. Cup in hand, he headed out the back door to sit on the steps and wait for the rising sun.

CHAPTER TWENTY-FIVE

Father Stephen Mario lay awake in the bedroom he had been assigned by Father Cameron the evening before, after the Bishop's heartbreaking revelation. The pain of the accusation broke his spirit like nothing before. His own congregation, whom he loved deeply, turned against him. He could have understood their concerns – had they been justified. But justified they were not. Why hadn't the parents of the boys come to him first? He was no threat to the young innocence of any minor, and certainly not to the boys in question.

Father Mario's room was in the back of the house and from his bed he saw the twilight forming shapes of nature outside his window – a big tree, with deep green leaves so thick that he couldn't see the sky beyond it. He listened for any sign of wakefulness in other parts of the house, but heard nothing to indicate that anyone – besides himself – was awake. Only the sounds of singing birds kept the silence from falling in on him.

He looked around the room in an attempt to find anything interesting enough to take his mind off all that had happened in the last 24 hours. He had visited Father Cameron many times at the Armstrong home, but he had never stayed overnight nor seen the upstairs.

His room was painted a buttery yellow with a dark stained oak crown molding. On one wall was a collection of three lithographs depicting a variety of garden plants in bloom. Although Father Mario was not a gardener, he did recognize – or thought he recognized – a lilac tree. It looked like a small tree he remembered from his youth that grew in the front yard and bloomed a heavenly scent in early spring. He thought back to those days as a small boy and remembered how the house would be filled with the scent of the blooms from the few small branches his mother would place in a vase on the center of their small dining table.

On the back wall were double windows over which hung a white lace and heavy drapes in a flowered print. The drapes were pulled away from the windows and held in place by bronze tie-backs that boasted what appeared to be dark leather ovals. He had not bothered to close the drapes the evening before when he came into his room, but rather sat for a long time on the side of the bed. His mind had been too tired to think, his body too tired to move. When he had nodded off to sleep sitting up, he had slipped off his slacks and shirt, folded them both neatly and placed them on the foot of the bed. Then in just his boxer shorts he had climbed under the sheets and drifted into a restless sleep.

Father Mario sat up in the bed and continued his exploration of the room. He had not noticed them last night but now, from the bed on which he sat, he noticed what appeared to be a collection of painted feathers.

He pushed back the covers, threw his legs over the side of the bed and allowed himself to be pulled by curiosity closer to the display cases. Inside each case were ten brown mottled feathers, each nearly a foot long, painted with intricate garden and wildlife scenes. He marveled at the details of each – the dragonfly hovering over a yellow butterfly bush, the hummingbird taking nectar from a feeder hung graciously over a wild tangle of colorful blooms.

He was fascinated by the artistic expression. For the ten minutes he allowed himself the pleasure of being mesmerized, he forgot his heartache. But when the detail of the last painted feather, a gray squirrel climbing down the trunk of a small tree, had been absorbed, he remembered where he was and how he had gotten there. Worse than that, he remembered the Bishop's conversation from the evening before, and the pain.

A sharp throb in his chest took his breath away. He backed himself up to the bed and sat. Father Mario placed his right hand over his heart and took a deep breath. *Easy,* he thought. *Keep this up and you're going to end up in the hospital again.* He practiced a deep breathing exercise he had learned in seminary to settle his mind. He knew that what he needed was focus. With focus he could set the hurt aside and analyze how best to vindicate himself from the accusations that were upon him. But even if he were successful, Father Mario questioned whether he could stay with the Church. At this point, he didn't even know if being a priest was the best way to spend his life. He hadn't been at it very long and already the worse kind of fate had fallen upon him – the accusation of inappropriate affection with two boys in the church – one of whom was now dead.

Separate yourself from the emotion; separate yourself from the emotion, he repeated to himself. *You must not let the Church down in this way, even though they have let you down.* Father Mario knew this self-talk would be the only way he could pull himself out of his self-pity and focus on the preservation of his oath to the Church. There were, in fact, many things riding on his ability to clear himself of any wrong-doing.

"I need some tea or coffee," he said out loud to the display of feathers on the wall. He reached for his clothes still neatly folded at the end of the bed and dressed. Looking around the room he realized there was no mirror. He ran his fingers through his brown hair and walked to the door, opening it as quietly as possible. Outside his room, someone had placed a TV tray that held a folded bath towel, hand towel and washcloth. A small basket next to the linens contained travel-sized hair shampoo and bath gel; and much to his pleasure, a new toothbrush and toothpaste.

Father Mario's eyes traveled across the hallway to where the Bishop had been appointed. He too, had a TV tray to the side of his door with the same provisions. But the Bishop's bedroom door stood open and Father Mario noticed the bed was made. He stepped quietly across the hall and stood inside the doorway. "Bishop Grogan?"

When no response came, Father Mario walked into the room and looked for any evidence of the Bishop having been there, but saw nothing. The bed was meticulously made, so either it had not been slept in or the Bishop was very expert on how to make a bed. He walked across the room and pulled back one of the sheer panels that hung in front of the window. Looking out over the driveway, he saw that the Bishop's car was gone. Apparently, the Bishop had some other place he needed to be.

CHAPTER TWENTY-SIX

Chief Johnson whistled as he walked into the police station the next morning at 0600 carrying a grocery bag. Always an early riser, he woke every morning at 0430 without the need of an alarm. This morning he'd nestled up close to Tanya, inhaling the smell of her skin and remembering their passion from the evening before. His lips found the lobe of her ear but she pushed him away with a loud grunt that he knew meant, *It's too early for me. Go away!*

He got up, started the coffee, showered and was out the door at 5:30. On the way, he stopped at Harris Teeter to grab some fruit and yogurt for the briefing he had scheduled for 0700. In his years of experience, he knew that the team came together better over food, so he grabbed bags of red and green apples, oranges and two large bunches of bananas. Wandering over to the dairy section, he added a dozen containers of yogurt and picked up several bags of string cheese.

The first time he had brought in such an offering, the guys laughed. *Fruit and string cheese? You've got to be kidding!* Chief had chided that he was going to erase the doughnut reputation and threatened that if he ever saw a patrol car in front of a doughnut shop without just cause, he'd dock them half a day's pay. Though several officers had privately challenged his authority to actually carry through with that threat, no one ever dared find out first hand.

The Chief placed the bag on the team table in the middle of the room and proceeded to the dispatcher's desk to review the shift report. Typical stuff, accidents with injury; car fire; two alarms set off, no indication of forced entry. *Pretty quiet,* the Chief thought... *Quiet before or after the storm,* he wondered. Though his evening with Tanya had been a wonderful respite from the Conner tragedy, his mind had never stopped considering, computing, analyzing. In fact, his mind never stopped, period.

He made a point of speaking to all the officers on the shift. It was important for him to know each of them, and he made a concerted effort to carve time out of each day to spend a few moments in dialog with them. Although many of them were finishing their night shift and ready to go home, he invited them to grab a piece of fruit or a yogurt. "There's enough for everyone, don't be shy," Chief Johnson said cheerfully.

In truth, the Chief knew that the more officers he had sitting around the table come time for the morning debrief, the more input he would get. That's just the way it worked, everyone had something to contribute – whether they were familiar with the case or not.

At 0645 the Chief's cell phone rang. He looked at the number and recognized it as Julia's. Stepping into his office and closing the door, he answered.

"Good morning, Sunshine. Found my dog yet?"

"Good morning to you too, Moonshine. You making a statement this morning at 0800?"

"No ma'am. I told you no statements yet. This is a pivotal time – got to make sure we're off in the right direction before we start folks talking."

"So, when can we talk about the missing dog?"

"I knew you'd come around to the dog story. And no one better than you to write such a moving story either."

"Oh shut up. Let's just stick to the facts and if the facts move the reader then so be it."

"How'd you get to be so cold? Too long without a good man?"

"I don't need no man so don't start on me. Right now all I need is a story. You have an entire family murdered in their own home and you got nothing to say about it."

"Come on Julia. You know how I work."

"Hmmm. And you know how I work. So what about this dog?"

Chief Johnson sighed. He needed Julia to understand how the dog was going to help them get traction on the case. He knew she took her work very seriously and that right now she was bringing herself down to the most elementary levels of newspaper journalism to write about a missing dog.

Through his office windows he saw officers Lacey and Zach come in. He knew they'd make their way over to the team table and rummage through the bag. Officer Lacey would be disappointed there weren't any sweets.

"Are you going to tell me anything about the dog or not?" Julia was losing patience. The Chief could only imagine how demanding a woman like her would be in bed. *No,* he thought. *I'm not going there, I'm not going there, I'm not going there.*

"Tell you what, Tinkerbell, let me call you back. Give me two hours and I'll give you all you need to know about the dog, okay?"

"You just like to make me wait."

"No, I just don't want to waste your time. I'll call you back." The Chief ended the call and rose from his desk. The team was assembling and they had a lot to get done today. Julia was right. The clock was ticking and there was no time to lose.

At the team table, several officers were picking through the offerings of fruit and yogurt and chatting among themselves about the Conner murders.

"Men, women," Chief Johnson started, always keen to ensure gender equality although he only had one female officer in the room. "Let's review where we are." He rolled over the dry erase board and picked up a handful of colored markers from the tray. Pulling the top off the red marker, he began framing the timing of the murders.

"This is what we know. At 0200 hours, Tuesday, July 19, a call came in to the dispatcher from an unknown source reporting a disturbance at the Conner residence. Do we know yet where the call came from?" The Chief turned around and was looking at Lieutenant Charley Eaton, an officer on the force as long as the Chief himself. Lieutenant Eaton was a short, burly man who wore his hair in a comb-over despite of years of merciless ridicule from the other officers.

"Yes, sir, the call came in from one of the three Conner cell phones. The caller sounds female and all she said was that there had been a disturbance at the Conner home. Then she gave the address. We went through the cell phone provider and traced the call to the closest tower; looks like Newport News-Williamsburg airport area. No further calls have been made from that number, and when I dial the number it goes directly into voicemail. We're speculating the phone is either off or has been destroyed. Interestingly, we've played the recording for several voice analysts and they all agree that it sounds like a female from the Southwest."

"Thanks, Eaton. If the call came from the airport at 0200, that's half an hour from the Conners' home with no traffic. So, if the perp was calling to report the murders, it had to have occurred before 0130. Any leads on the woman? Any connections to someone from... What is considered Southwest? Texas, Nevada?"

"Arizona, New Mexico, Oklahoma, and Texas," Zach sang in a catchy jingle. "I had to memorize the states by regions in the fifth grade. Haven't been able to forget the song that goes along with it either."

"You've remembered it for a whole year," George Lacey muttered, loud enough for all to hear. An uproar of laughter broke out.

"Okay, that's enough!" Chief Johnson boomed, but he too had laughed. He looked over at Zach, "Man, I thought the song was beautiful. You're proving to be an excellent addition to the force."

Zach wasn't sure if the Chief was making fun or not, but he was proud of himself for answering the Chief's question. He puffed out his chest and nodded appreciatively. Beside him several officers turned their smiling faces into their coffee cups.

Chief Johnson noticed that Sergeant Walker was the only one who did not find the moment humorous. "Any connections to one of those states? *Arizona, New Mexico, Oklahoma and Texas,"* the Chief sang to the group, trying out the jingle.

"No, sir. Not yet," said Investigator Lacey, still smiling. "We're interviewing neighbors about recent visitors, anything that might help. All we've got so far is that the Conners had a woman coming out occasionally to help Mrs. Conner with the housework. Apparently while they were away for the week of the fourth of July, this woman stayed in the home to care for the dog."

"Do we know who this woman is, where she came from?"

"We're working on it, Sir. One neighbor thought she came from the Conners' church."

"Make that a priority," the Chief said, his mind thinking back to the eight parishioners he'd interviewed the night before and those who had slipped out the back door while he was negotiating with Sarah Pulley.

"So, let's talk about the dog. Did anyone at the house yesterday see anything to indicate a dog lived there?" Chief Johnson looked around to see all head's shaking.

"Sir, we did a thorough search of the front and back yards and I swear I don't ever remember seeing any dog shit. Maybe they trained the dog to shit in the pot or they always walked behind it with a pooper-scooper. All I know is we didn't see no signs of a dog."

"Thanks, Michaels. Seems strange that there would be nothing to indicate the presence of a dog. Even an inside dog's gotta go somewhere. Was this some prize champion dog from Westminster, or what?"

Again, nothing but shaking heads.

"Chief, I called over to forensics late yesterday and they did find black hair deep in the carpet throughout the house – more so in Mr. and Mrs. Conner's bedroom, on the inside right arm of the sofa and on the footstool in front of the picture window at the front of the house," Sergeant Walker said. "Too soon to confirm if it's dog hair, but none of the Conner family had black hair and it didn't appear to be pubic. They also found synthetic hair, so when we go back over today we'll look through the closets for a wig. Otherwise, if this proves to be hair from a wig, and Mrs. Conner doesn't own a wig, that could be an additional lead."

"Interesting. What else? Let's talk about the video, have you all reviewed it?" Heads nodded the affirmative and the Chief looked back over to Sergeant Walker.

"The video was made with the Kodak pocket video camera that was left connected to the computer in the kitchen. When I saw the camera next to the computer, I tapped the space bar and the computer came out of sleep mode with the video prompted to play. We sent a copy out for a psych eval, and the doc said Mrs. Conner didn't seem to have any fear in pulling the trigger. She was likely in such a state of shock that death would have been easier than living."

The last sentence was difficult for Sergeant Walker to get out without becoming emotional. While several heads dropped in compassion when they heard his voice crack, the two officers who were in the Conner house with him yesterday looked at each other and smirked.

"What would the motive be for video taping Mrs. Conner's suicide/murder?" Lieutenant Eaton asked. "It doesn't add up. You'd think if it was to boast, the killer would have taped the whole thing. Why just Mrs. Conner?"

Chief Johnson looked around the room, waiting for possible theories. "Someone speak up!" he said, demanding his team to think.

"The killer wanted to save the best for last," came a response from the back.

"It was too risky to get the first four on tape," offered Zach. "When there was just one left, the killer felt safe enough to play with the victim."

"Maybe it's like having sex with the lights off," Lacey said. "The perp likes it better in the dark, but sometimes you're forced to shed some light on it." The room filled with laughter and off-color remarks about any woman having sex with George Lacey would insist the lights be off.

Chief Johnson let the ruckus continue momentarily while he worked the puzzle in his mind. "Okay folks, listen up. You are having way too much fun this morning. Now you know why I don't allow doughnuts." He gave the room a minute to settle. "Let's think about this... Any evidence of sexual motives?"

"No," came the reply from several investigators.

"Care to elaborate?" the Chief asked.

"All victims were clothed, no sexual fluids found on the bodies or anywhere else at the scene," Eaton offered. "At least nothing prelim coming from forensics to suggest otherwise."

"No signs of bondage that might suggest sexual fantasies," Michaels added.

"Anything to suggest these murders could be related to past crimes?" the Chief asked.

"We're looking into that," Investigator Lacey said. "I've got our computer guru running some searches – should know by lunch time if there are any hits."

"Let's go back to the murder/suicide," Chief Johnson said. "There's something there, I just can't pin it. Power and control? Vendetta? C'mon, there's gotta be something there. The fact that the killer left the video ready to play means they wanted it to be seen. Was it to suggest the accomplishment of a great feat?"

The Chief let the question sit for a minute before continuing. "What about the murder weapon. What can we tell from the video? Do we know if the Conner family owned a gun and if so, is it missing? Do we think the same weapon was used on all the victims?" The Chief's eyes scanned the room and then paused on Sergeant Walker.

"Mrs. Conner held the gun in her left hand and when we enlarged the video we could see the S&W insignia on the barrel; single-action, .22 double revolver – we dug the bullet out of the wall between the living room and the kitchen. Not the same sized ammo found in the room of the children and Mr. Conner – 9 mm in all cases. So, we're looking at two weapons, neither of which was found at the scene. My guess is that the killer was holding a gun on Mrs. Conner and would have killed her had she not killed herself. We've looking into state and federal registration databases for anything registered by the Conner family."

Chief Johnson was in deep thought, considering the facts. He crossed his arms over his chest, and twirled the marker he held in his right. "Okay... Let's go back to the dog," he prompted. "Have we checked the dog shelters, city pound, asked neighbors?"

"I've called all the rescue shelters and the city," Zach offered. "Lots of black dogs, but no cocker spaniels. We're going back to the house to look for photos today."

"Good, we'll need them," the Chief agreed. "I've got a gut feeling that this dog is going to be our best ticket to a good lead. When you folks are out talking to neighbors, ask if the dog was a barker. If so, he would have barked in the middle of the night at a stranger. Someone might have heard it. If he didn't bark, he must have known the perp. And don't forget to ask if the dog was potty trained," the Chief added with a smile. "Oh, and before I forget, our favorite newspaper guru, Julia Frank, will be coming by later today to get the story on the dog. We'll probably be running a feature piece on the missing dog in tomorrow's paper."

"Was that what she was calling me for last night?" asked Lacey. "She called the dispatcher half a dozen times but I wouldn't take the call. God I hope she never gets my cell number."

"I've no idea what she was calling you about last night, Lacey," the Chief said. "Last I heard she was single and free and so are you."

Chief Johnson let the laughter die down before continuing in a more serious tone. "If she calls again, you'll need to talk to her – but only as far as the dog is concerned. If she's pushing for anything else, shut her down. She wants an official statement, of course. I'd like to make a statement late tonight or early morning so let's see what we can get today. I want a team out near the airport looking around. Let's think about how we might locate that phone. Anything else?"

"What about the possible connection between the cleaning lady slash house-sitter and the church?" asked Zach.

"Glad you asked. Sergeant Walker and I were at St. Joseph's yesterday afternoon and interviewed several members of a group who were apparently trying to oust Father Mario for what had been reported by a couple of teen boys as inappropriate affection. Several members who signed the petition slipped out before we could talk to them. We've got the church assistant pulling all the names for us. We'll head back over there first thing this morning. There are a few church staff, including our friend Father Mario, whom we'll be speaking to. Anything else?"

"Can you get more strawberry and banana yogurt next time?" asked Lieutenant Eaton. "I really appreciate the gesture and the peach is okay, but a little variety would be nice. And, I am trying to slim down a bit."

"You got it, anything to help you trim down," the Chief said, smiling. "All right, if there's nothing else, everybody chop-chop! Walker, you're with me," he said reaching into the bag for the string cheese but finding none. "Damn," he said under his breath. "That's my favorite!"

"Chief, I think you'll want to hear this." Lacey said, walking over to the table where Chief Johnson continued to rummage through the bag for the string cheese.

"What 'cha got?"

"Missing person report."

Lacey had the Chief's attention now. "Yes, let's have it."

"Sixteen year old Kevin Larson, best friend of Michael Conner, the oldest of the Conner children. His mother didn't find him this morning when they went to wake him for breakfast. She thought maybe he'd not been able to sleep and was out in the garage or the yard. When she couldn't find him she tried calling his cell phone but didn't get an answer."

Chief Johnson listened as Investigator Lacey gave him the details. He stood quietly for a moment considering the possible implications. "Doesn't sound good," he finally concluded. "Get Walker and let's head over to the Larson's home. Tell your buddy Zach to pull together a search party. We might need one."

CHAPTER TWENTY-SEVEN

Bishop Grogan had not slept well. Even in sleep the past, present and future had disturbed him. He knew he needed counsel – someone he trusted – someone who would understand. It was easier to leave the house before anyone awakened; no explanation would be needed, no breakfast offerings to consider. Father Cameron was a generous host. Margaret's dinner had been excellent, but difficult to enjoy knowing the news he'd have to deliver afterwards.

Bishop Grogan considered Father Cameron the luckiest of any priest he knew – a lovely small middle-class parish and a beautiful home complete with cook, housekeeper and errand runner – all a mysterious gift to the Church by a non-Catholic. *Go figure.* The thought of it made him long for what he considered the simplicity of Father Cameron's daily life. *But even he's affected now,* Bishop Grogan thought, *considering that his best friend has been accused of such a ghastly sin.* The Bishop didn't believe Father Mario to be guilty, but he didn't know what Father Cameron was thinking or even how much he really knew.

The Bishop turned his Cadillac into the parking lot of St. Joseph's and shut off the engine. For a couple of moments he sat in silent, reflective prayer, *Dear God, let the truth be known whatever that truth may be. Help me keep straight on the road of righteousness. May I put the Church and the people always before my own needs, second only to Thy will, oh Lord most high. Amen.*

His sighed deeply and opened the car door. Pulling his brief case from the passenger seat, he headed toward the small parish house behind the church. Through the window he saw a warm, yellow light and suspected that Father Patrick was already up and about. His suspicion was confirmed when Father Patrick quickly opened the door.

"Why Bishop Grogan, what a lovely surprise. Come in, come in!"

"Thank you Father Patrick. I'm so glad to know I didn't wake you at this hour."

"Now Bishop, how long have we known each other?" Both men chuckled as Father Patrick motioned the Bishop through the living room and into the small kitchen.

"Care for a cup of English tea?" Father Patrick asked, reaching for two cups from the cupboard. "As an Irishman I should refrain from the British temptation, but what can I say. The Brits cornered the market on good tea – that they did!"

Bishop Grogan took one of the two stools at the kitchen counter and nodded his head in understanding. He sat quietly while Father Patrick shuffled around the kitchen chatting about his early days in Belfast. A few moments later the whistle from the kettle pierced the air and tea was served.

CHAPTER TWENTY-EIGHT

It was just past morning rush hour when the station wagon pulled back onto 95 heading south. In the back, inside the metal pet carrier, a dog whimpered, then gave out a high-pitched howl which ended in a series of soft barks. Again and again, the dog cried out.

Earlier in the trip, the voice from the front offered reassurances. Now, loud singing was the only response:

In God I put my trust

My Father so near

He guides me wherever I go

He is waiting at the gates

With wide open arms

He's calling, yes, calling me home

CHAPTER TWENTY-NINE

Father Cameron headed back into the house for a second cup of coffee and met Father Mario looking around for the cups.

"Coffee or tea?" he asked, wondering how well his friend was holding up.

"Coffee's fine," Father Mario answered, hints of melancholy in his voice.

Father Cameron opened a cupboard and took out a coffee cup and placed it on the counter. "Milk or sugar?"

"I'm good," Father Mario said, picking up the cup and filling it with coffee.

"I can't even begin to imagine how difficult all of this is for you," Father Cameron began.

Father Mario looked into his cup and nodded appreciatively. "I hardly know what to think," he answered softly. "Honestly, my mind doesn't want to think no matter how hard I try to focus."

There was so much Father Cameron wanted to say, questions he wanted to ask, but he felt uncertain. Instead, he reached out his hand and placed it firmly on Father Mario's shoulder. "You know I'm here for you, Steve. You only need to tell me how I can best support you – as friend or as priest."

Father Mario nodded. "If I only knew what to ask for..." his voice dropped and the sentence hung unfinished.

The two men stood in the quiet of the kitchen sipping from their cups but saying nothing. It was a relief to both when Margaret joined them to begin her morning routine. "Good morning Fathers. What would the two of you wish for breakfast? How about eggs, ham and biscuits? It shouldn't take any time to serve it up," she said as she fastened the apron around her spreading waist.

"Sounds wonderful," Father Cameron answered, looking to Father Mario for input.

"Yes, indeed," he answered, trying a smile. "Just wonderful."

CHAPTER THIRTY

Father Patrick expected that Bishop Grogan wanted to talk about something important but he didn't press. In his many years, one thing he had learned was how to wait – after all, all things come to those who wait, so why rush?

Bishop Grogan listened as Father Patrick reflected back on his childhood and the hardships that being born to a poor laboring family brought. He knew the story well, having often heard Father Patrick's telling of Irish Catholic history. He didn't mind the retellings as it entertained him to hear the variations in Father Patrick's storytelling. On one occasion, he is the distant relative of a slain Catholic priest – killed at the merciless hands of the Protestant Orangemen in the early 1800s. In another telling, he's the fourth cousin, thrice removed from the famous Daniel O'Connell, known in history books as the Catholic emancipator.

Those details really did not matter to Father Patrick. What was important were the details that never wavered – the history around how the Irish Catholics were divested of their lands; not allowed to hold public office nor vote in elections; were forbidden to marry Protestants and, if they did, the local Protestant government would immediately annul them and hang the priest who conducted the ceremony. These were the details that never changed, as they were the truth that had been told from father to son and from mother to daughter for hundreds of years.

It was no surprise then that the man who was now Father Patrick held his Irish heritage so passionately. Its history of suffering in the name of religion had fated generations of Irish families to lives of destitution and ignorance – and had inspired him as a young lad to become a Catholic priest in spite of it all.

Sitting now at the kitchen counter, Bishop Grogan listened to his friend, the strong accent of his ancestry sounding in his ears like a Celtic song. These words gave him strength and inspiration and he sat quietly and listened until Father Patrick finally stopped, his blue eyes resting curiously on the Bishop. For a moment, Bishop Grogan thought perhaps he'd missed something. "I'm sorry?" he asked, returning Father Patrick's intent gaze.

"I've said naught a word in the last five minutes, Bishop," Father Patrick replied. "I was waiting to see if you wanted another tea."

"Oh yes, thank you," Bishop Grogan said, quickly raising his cup. "I must have been lost in the thought of persecution – I was listening you know." He smiled at the elder priest who looked at the Bishop over his shoulder. "You were telling me that the Irish Catholics were not permitted to own land and that they couldn't hold a lease for more than 31 years." Bishop smiled broadly, hoping his repeat of the lesson was accurate.

"Aye, you were listening then, weren't you?"

"Aye indeed," the Bishop replied, in his best Irish brogue.

"Persecution, for whatever reason, is such tragedy. But I'll always believe the worse tragedy lies in persecution on the grounds of religion. Did you know, Bishop, that in the 1800s if a child of a Catholic professed him or herself to be a Protestant that the child would be immediately taken from the parent's care and placed into a Protestant home? And, that the family was then required to pay child support for the child that was no longer considered theirs?"

Bishop Grogan listened but his mind had stopped on Father Patrick's statement about religious persecution. It brought up many emotions from his upbringing and played a large part in his current turmoil.

Father Patrick returned to his stool and, having placed Bishop Grogan's cup gently in its saucer, rested his gaze upon the Bishop, waiting.

Bishop Grogan sighed deeply, knowing that this telling would be difficult. He looked at the clock on the wall and then cleared his throat loudly. "There is something I'd like to chat with you about – as a longtime friend. It's a burden I've carried for many years, not of outright guilt, but guilt by association, of sorts. I've thought many times over that I'd forgiven myself, but I realize after all these years that I remain unforgiven." Bishop Grogan looked at his friend for understanding and saw in the blue eyes a sense of unconditional trust and acceptance.

Father Patrick said nothing, but nodded his head gently as if encouraging Bishop Grogan to go on. Once again Bishop Grogan sighed deeply, his heavy chest rising so much so that Father Patrick wondered how any man could inhale so much oxygen in one breath.

"I don't think I've ever told you that I had a younger brother, two years my junior?" He asked the question, knowing already the answer. He watched as Father Patrick's eyes widened in interest and his head shook from side to side.

"Yes, he was my only sibling and from the time I can remember, he was a gentle soul. Gentle, but different. When we were younger I guess I really didn't notice so much, but when we were in grade school, his differences became a burden to me. The other kids always made fun of him yet I never defended him. Instead, I chastised him and told him to toughen up. By the time we were in high school, it was very clear that my brother – Jeremy was his name – was very different." Bishop Grogan looked to Father Patrick to see if there was understanding, but Father Patrick's face remained without judgment or apparent recognition of what "different" meant.

"Jeremy liked boys." Bishop Grogan said, wincing at the words. He hung his head for a long moment before meeting Father Patrick's eyes. "But that's not the worst thing..." Bishop Grogan said, his voice cracking as he searched for the right words.

Father Patrick reached out and placed his hand on the Bishop's arm, "It's okay, go on..."

The Bishop's face twisted with the pain of memories and trying to put the past into words. "The worse of it is me," he managed to get out. "It was autumn. I had just come home from football practice and the guys had been hammering me the whole time about my brother. When I got home I was so angry with him that I lashed out at him and told him how ashamed he made the family and that I wished he'd leave home and never come back."

135

Father Patrick watched tears form in the Bishop's eyes, his heart aching from the deeply suppressed memories. He knew then that the story about to unfold was tragic, and Father Patrick braced himself.

As Bishop Grogan met Father Patrick's eyes, his chin trembled with the words that stuck in his throat until finally the ending tumbled out. "My father found him the next morning hanging from a tree in our back yard. He'd left a note for us telling us how sorry he was for all the shame he'd brought upon us. He said he just didn't know how better to end it all and asked that we forgive him. My parents never knew about our altercation the day before. After Jeremy's death they poured all of their love into me. I never told anyone... until now." Bishop Grogan's whole body convulsed as the story came to its ending, his large frame collapsing onto the table as he succumbed to a long repressed grief.

Father Patrick stood and placed his arms around the broken Bishop and began to rock him gently. From somewhere in the depths of his memory he heard his mother's voice singing and his own voice found the words which he now sang.

Turn thee unto me, oh, Lord, turn thee unto me

Turn thee unto me, oh, Lord, your love has set me free

CHAPTER THIRTY-ONE

Julia Frank looked at her watch – two hours had passed since her morning chat with Chief Johnson. *Damn him*, she thought. *Playing me again...* She reached for her iPhone and pulled up her contacts list, pushed J, scrolled until she found Chief Johnson's name and pressed the call button. Seconds later, he picked up.

"Ladybug, I can't talk with you right now, new turn in the story. How about I call you when we're free and you can meet me and a couple of my men for coffee. We'll catch up there."

"Which men?" she asked, clearly unhappy with the continuance.

"Lacey and Walker."

"Do I get to bop Lacey over the head for ignoring my calls yesterday? I'm not stupid."

"We all know you're not stupid. Call you soon, doll baby."

Julia hated when the Chief called her pet names, but she knew that for some men, the use of familiar names made them feel closer to women. And Chief Johnson was someone she needed to be close to if she was going to continue to write award-winning news; and, if ultimately she was going to move to a prominent paper like the New York Times or the Wall Street Journal. She could put up with a few pet names.

Her outline for the dog story was taking shape. She had made several calls to dog trainers and in just twenty minutes phone time, felt like she had a good idea of how Calvin, the cocker spaniel would be acting if he was still alive and had, in fact, witnessed his family's brutal murder. She hoped that coffee wouldn't run late; she had a 1300 meeting with one of the trainers who offered to introduce her to a couple of cocker spaniels. Though she didn't care for animals of any kind, for this story she was going to love them.

Besides, if she did this dog story for the Chief, he would owe her. Big time.

CHAPTER THIRTY-TWO

When the two police cars pulled into the Larson's drive, Kevin's mother Jenny was pacing the sidewalk between the driveway and the steps leading up to the front door. She was petite, with shortly cropped brown hair, and dressed in khaki shorts and a yellow t-shirt that read *Kecoughtan High School Rocks*. She ran to greet the first officer that emerged from the vehicle – Chief Johnson.

"Are you Mrs. Larson?"

"Yes, officer, I am the one who called in to report my son Kevin missing. I've just got the worst feeling about this. Please tell me you can help find him," she pleaded, tears streaming down her face.

"We'll do everything we can, ma'am. I'm Police Chief Carl Johnson and this is Sergeant Walker and Investigator Lacey," he said, as the two men approached. "Can we step inside? We'd like to ask you some questions and, if we could, take a look through Kevin's room."

"Yes, of course – I just have a bad feeling, a really bad

feeling." Jenny repeated as she led the officers up the steps and into the living room.

They waited respectfully for Mrs. Larson to indicate where they should sit, but she continued pacing the floor. Finally Chief Johnson stepped forward and placed his hands squarely on her shoulders and waited for her to look him in the eyes. "Mrs. Larson, you indicated that you have a really bad feeling. Can you tell us why?"

"I can't explain it. I just feel... so scared."

"I can't imagine how frightened you must feel right now," Chief Johnson responded. "In my experience, the quicker we start searching, the better chance we have of finding your son. I need you to take a deep breath and put your fears aside and tell us what happened. We've got an officer back at the station pulling together a search party as we speak. I can't tell you how this will end, but I can tell you that we are here to help you. We need you to help us first. Now, let's sit and you can tell us everything you know."

When everyone was settled, Chief Johnson turned again to Jenny. "Mrs. Larson, let's start from the beginning. When you called the station this morning, you indicated that Kevin and Michael Conner were best friends and that Kevin was distraught over the family's murder, which seems only natural. Can you describe his behavior for us in as much detail as possible?"

Jenny Larson nodded her head and closed her eyes as if rewinding her mental tape. Eyes still closed, she spoke slowly and softly so that all the men leaned forward, straining to hear her.

"Yesterday morning the kids were still sleeping at 10:30, when I finally had a moment to open the paper. I couldn't believe my eyes. Then the phone rang. It was Sarah Pulley from our church. She said that Liza Morris, who lives a couple of blocks over from the Conner family, walked over to their house after she saw the morning paper. Liza told Sarah the police cordoned the house off and the squad cars and emergency vehicles were everywhere. Sarah told me that a special session of our committee was going to be held."

Sarah paused, then looked back up at Chief Johnson. "I'm sorry I ran out of the church yesterday. I saw you and the other officer come in, but I..." she paused again before continuing, "I needed to get home to start dinner for my husband. He likes to eat when he gets home from work. He's always so hungry," she laughed nervously.

"Let's not worry about that, Mrs. Larson," Chief Johnson said, wanting to ease her mind. He made a mental note to come back to her involvement in the church committee later. Right now, he just needed her to focus on telling them about Kevin and his friendship with the Conner boy. "So, Mrs. Pulley confirmed the news in the paper. What did you do then?"

Again, Jenny closed her eyes, rewound her words to the phone call and took her mental recorder off pause. "After I got off the phone with Sarah, I called my husband at work and told him the news. I didn't realize that Kevin had come out of his room and was standing at the kitchen pantry. I guess he was looking for the cereal. Anyway, he heard me tell my husband about the murders." Again she paused, sighed deeply as new tears streamed down her face, and continued. "He ran up to me and grabbed me and started shaking me demanding that I deny what I'd just said. I could hear my husband yelling in the phone but I couldn't answer him because Kevin was shaking me so hard. I dropped the phone and started trying to calm him down. He was hysterical, screaming at me and talking crazy stuff."

Chief Johnson interrupted, "What kind of crazy stuff, Mrs. Larson. Every detail is important."

She looked sadly at the Chief and shook her head. "I'm sorry, I really can't remember."

"That's okay," the Chief said soothingly. "Go on. Then what happened?"

"His sister Caroline heard him yelling and came out of her room. She was trying to get him to let go of me. She was screaming at him. Everyone was screaming..." She dropped her head into her hands. "It was awful."

"So he let go of you?" the Chief asked, urging her on.

"Yes, he let go and ran back to his room. Caroline and I were sitting at the table talking quietly about what had happened when he came back. He was dressed and demanded that I give him the car keys. He just got his license a few weeks ago, but he wasn't supposed to drive without an adult in the car – our rules. I told him I'd take him wherever he needed to go, but he was hovering over me – I was afraid, I didn't know what to do. I told him the keys were in my purse on my bedroom dresser. He went back to my room to get the keys and I asked Caroline if she would go with him. When he came back out he was practically running to the car. Caroline went after him but he pushed her to the ground and locked the doors to the car so she couldn't get in. That's the last we saw of him."

Chief Johnson sat quietly, respectful of Jenny's concern and pain. He watched as she wiped the fresh stream of tears from her face and took a tissue from her pocket and blew her nose. He didn't like how this story sounded, he'd heard similar stories before and they never seemed to end nicely. "Mrs. Larson, it would be good if we could also speak to your husband and daughter. Are there any other children in the home?"

"No other children, just Caroline and she's still sleeping. My husband is at work."

"Does your husband know that Kevin didn't come home last night?" the Chief asked, surprised that the husband would have gone to work knowing that his son was missing.

Mrs. Larson hesitated before answering. "Yes. He was very angry that Kevin took the car and he drove around the neighborhood looking for him last night. When he wasn't home this morning, my husband said that he would come home when he got hungry."

Chief Johnson thought about all the 16 year old kids he'd known to run off and never come home. *Yep,* he thought. *I've heard this story before.* "Would you mind waking Caroline? Perhaps we can take a look in Kevin's room and that will give her enough time to get the sleepy out of her eye," he said, trying to sound casual about the request.

Mrs. Larson stood and headed down the hallway. "This way," she said. "I'll show you Kevin's room." Suddenly she spun around to face the three men following her. "You're not going to take anything are you?" she asked, as if the room was all she had left of her son.

"No ma'am, not unless we ask you first. We're just going to look around for any clue to where he might have gone," the Chief reassured her.

When Mrs. Larson left the room to wake Caroline, the Chief closed the door behind her. "Okay, the usual routine. I'm going to try to get a little more out of Mrs. Larson about the church committee. I'll ask the same questions we asked the other members yesterday. You two find whatever you can in here and then you can join me out front."

"I don't see any signs of a computer," Investigator Lacey said, looking around. "Either he took it or the family shares a computer in another part of the house."

"Yes, we definitely need to find out what computer he would have used. I'll work on that while you two look through here."

Chief Johnson opened the door and stepped back into the hallway. Emerging from the bathroom on the other side of the hallway was a girl who he guessed to be Caroline. She was taller than her mother and athletically built. Her long strawberry-blond hair had just been brushed and several long strands around her face levitated with static. Her green eyes were large and puffy and he imagined she had been crying.

"Caroline?" he asked gently.

"Yes, sir?"

"I'm Chief Johnson. Can we sit down in the living room? I'm hoping you can help me find your brother."

Caroline nodded and walked toward the living room. As they passed the door to the kitchen the Chief saw Mrs. Larson on the phone. *Did I hear a phone ring or did she call out? She must have called out.* Chief hesitated then stood in the doorway until Mrs. Larson hung up. "Everything okay?"

"Yes, I was just speaking to my husband. I told him you wanted to talk to him but he says he can't leave work right now.

Can he talk to you later?"

"Yes, of course," the Chief said, making a mental note. "Mrs. Larson, would you mind joining Caroline and me in the living room? I'd like for you to be present while I talk to her."

CHAPTER THIRTY-THREE

"Have you ever been in love?" Father Mario asked. He and Father Cameron had moved from the kitchen to the picture window in the study, where they stood looking out at the garden.

Father Cameron was surprised by the question. Although they had known each other since seminary, the topic of being in love had never come up. He thought for a moment before answering. "Yes. Haven't you?"

"What was she like?" Father Mario pressed on, ignoring the question.

Father Cameron's heart lurched, not at the thought of his past love but at the thought of his past sin. The love was painful enough, but now – many years later and given his vocation – it was painful and shameful. He looked at his friend and saw a sad man. Father Cameron considered the previous day and the pain and shame that Father Mario was enduring in this very moment. He realized that, although the circumstances were very different, they both carried burdens in their hearts.

"When I first started teaching in North Georgia, I fell in love with a married woman. I didn't know she was married until after we were already involved. She told me because she was returning to her husband after spending the summer caring for her aunt who lived in the town where I was teaching. I was devastated. Not that she was married but that she was leaving me to go back to him." Father Cameron paused, in reflection. "Well, that's what she said anyway. After all this time, I guess I really don't know the truth."

"At least you've been in love," Father Mario answered after a long pause. "I'm not sure I know what that feels like. I thought I was in love with Christ and the Church, but I don't know what I feel anymore."

Father Cameron turned and seated himself behind his desk. He swiveled in his chair to face Father Mario and fought to find the right words. "It's perfectly understandable that you would feel confused about your relationship with Christ and the Church given the last twenty-four hours. God is testing your faith, my friend."

"God is winning," came the sharp reply. "What was her name?"

"What?" asked Father Cameron, momentarily confused.

"The married woman, what was her name?"

"Liz – short for Elizabeth. Elizabeth Grant."

"What did you do to get over her?"

"I grew bitter and lived miserably; then I went into the seminary. Looking back, I realize I wasted a huge part of my life wallowing in self-pity. Yet the experience, as painful and humiliating as it was, somehow led me to the Church. Now I couldn't begin to imagine what my life would be like if I weren't a priest."

Father Mario watched as Father Cameron leaned forward

with his elbows on his knees and stared at the floor. He walked over and sat in one of the chairs facing the desk, the subtle leather making a soft whoosh as he sat back. "Do you still have the files?"

"Yes," Father Cameron answered, without needing clarification.

"Can I see them? It's been a while and if we're going to be talking to the police, I'd like to have another look to refresh my memory."

Father Cameron turned his chair, opened the file drawer to the left of his desk and moved the hanging files forward until he could easily reach the file at the back. He pulled it out and placed it on the desk in front of Father Mario who didn't hesitate to pick it up. He opened the file and let his eyes rest on the first page.

"So much hate in the world – so much judgment," he mumbled. "Such a shame."

CHAPTER THIRTY-FOUR

Caroline and her mother sat next to each other on the sofa and the Chief took the chair nearest them. Caroline looked at him expectantly while her mother reached over and attempted to settle her fly-away hair. "Caroline, I know this must be hard for you," the Chief began. "Your mom told me about what happened yesterday when Kevin overheard the news about the Conner family. How long had Kevin and Michael been friends?"

Caroline looked over at her mother as she tried to calculate when the Conners' joined St. Joseph's, which was the time they first became acquainted. After a moment's thought, Caroline looked back to Chief and told him Kevin and Michael had been friends for about four years.

"Did Kevin and Michael hang out a lot, or did they just see each other at church? Did they have a group of friends that they liked to chill with?"

Again Caroline looked at her mother who nodded her head as if to encourage Caroline's answer. "Usually, they would just hang out at each other's house. Sometimes here, sometimes at the

Conners'. They didn't really hang out with anyone else."

"So, if I went around the neighborhood and started asking kids to tell me about Kevin, what kind of things would they say?"

Caroline's face became unmistakably frightened and for a third time she looked to her mom. Mrs. Larson's eyes darted from daughter to the Chief. "Is that really necessary?" Mrs. Larson asked.

Chief Johnson considered Caroline's apparent discomfort along with Mrs. Larson's question. He was beginning to recognize a pattern of behavior he'd seen many times before in families who were in denial. He carefully chose what would be his final question for her. "Caroline, I'm going to ask you a very important question. It's also very personal and I want you to look right here in my eyes and give me an answer." He held his right hand in front of his face, pointing two fingers at his eyes. "Can you do that?"

She shuffled uncomfortably. "Yes," she answered.

"Okay, right here," he said again, reinforcing the eye contact with his hand. "Is there anything I need to know about your brother that you might be afraid or embarrassed to tell me?"

Caroline's eyes grew wide and just as she began to turn toward her mother she heard the Chief's voice, "Uh, uh, uh. You promised. Right here!" His fingers were again directing Caroline's eyes to his. She looked at the floor and studied the rug, appearing suddenly fragile.

"What kind of question is that," Mrs. Larson said. "How can that help you find my son?"

Chief Johnson didn't look at Mrs. Larson, nor did he respond to her question. Instead he leaned his head down closer to

Caroline's. "Caroline, you promised."

Slowly Caroline raised her eyes to meet his. "I guess I thought he was pretty stupid most of the time, just because he was younger than me. But isn't that normal with brothers and sisters?"

Although the Chief's full attention was on Caroline, it did not escape him that Mrs. Larson let out a deep breath. "I think you are absolutely right Caroline. Most brothers and sisters are like that. In fact, I can remember thinking my younger brother was from another galaxy for a long time."

Caroline forced a smile and began rubbing her bare feet back and forth on the rug.

"As I promised, that's my last question for you – well, at least for now," he said, smiling.

"Can I go?" she asked anxiously.

"Sure. I bet you're hungry for some breakfast," he answered. She nodded and was quickly off the sofa headed for the kitchen. Chief Johnson looked at Mrs. Larson. Her eyes teared up again as she waited for him to say something. When they heard Investigator Lacey and Sergeant Walker coming out of Kevin's room, they both looked down the hallway expectantly.

Sergeant Walker carried a couple of photos and some computer disks. He held them out for Mrs. Larson to see. "Ma'am, may we borrow these photos for a day or two? We need to have a good photo to use when we put out an APB."

She reached for the photos and looked at them. One was of Kevin sitting at the kitchen table. Mrs. Larson remembered taking the photo before school this past spring. He was wearing a green polo, which set off his hazel eyes, and his short brown hair was gelled up into spikes. Looking at the second photo, Mrs.

Larson appeared startled. "Where did you find this one? I've never seen it." Her hands were visibly shaking as she brought the photo closer.

"It was under his bedside lamp, along with a couple of other photos," Sergeant Walker replied. "By the way, cute dog. Is it yours?"

In this photo, Kevin and Michael were sitting on the back steps of the Conner home with Calvin in between them. Their arms were draped comfortably over each other while scratching Calvin's long ears. Both boys were smiling broadly and looked happy and peaceful. Mrs. Larson felt her emotions surging forth from deep within. As she handed the photos back to Sergeant Walker, she wondered who had taken the photo of Kevin and Michael together. "The dog belonged to the Conners – I think his name was Calvin. Kevin loved that dog and we've never had one; my husband wouldn't allow it. It's okay for you to take the photos, but of course I want them back when you're done."

"Yes, ma'am, of course," Sergeant Walker replied. "We'd also like to take these computer disks, in case there is anything on them that could be helpful. By the way, did Kevin have a computer?"

"He didn't have a personal computer, we didn't allow that," she said, nervously eyeing the disks. "We share a family computer in the kitchen."

"Can we have a quick look at it?" Investigator Lacey asked.

Mrs. Larson took a deep breath, which made the Chief doubt that he would like her response. "It wasn't working right last night and my husband took it in to work with him today to fix it. He works for GTech Networks in Buckroe Beach, so he knows all about that stuff."

The three men exchanged a questioning glance, and Sergeant Walker continued his questions. "Did Kevin have an iPod that provided internet access?"

"No, he didn't have any of those computer gadgets."

"You said he had a cell phone. Did he have texting or email on his phone?"

"I'm not sure," she answered slowly. "I don't really know. My husband set up all the phone plans."

All roads seemed to be going nowhere. "Would you mind giving us Kevin's cell phone number?" the Chief asked, reaching into his breast pocket for his notepad.

"Yes, of course," she answered, giving them a ten-digit number.

All three men jotted the number as she recited it to them. Chief Johnson scribbled a moment more before tearing off the lower half the page and handing it to Mrs. Larson. "This is my cell phone. I want you to call me if you hear or need anything."

Mrs. Larson took the number and nodded her thanks. "I just have a bad feeling about this. I don't know why, I just do."

Chief Johnson knew, as did the other officers, that a mother's intuition was acute. There wasn't much about this situation that gave the Chief any sense of hope. "Mrs. Larson, I almost forgot," he said. "About the church meeting yesterday. Do you believe Father Mario is guilty?"

At the question, Mrs. Larson visibly flinched. She shook her head back and forth before answering. "I just don't know what to think anymore. I just don't know."

CHAPTER THIRTY-FIVE

At 9:40 a.m. the green station wagon swerved across the second lane on the expressway and then quickly pulled off the road. Immediately the driver's side door opened and vomit spewed forth as passing cars slowed to rubber-neck. Although the driver had all the windows open, the smell of the stench coming from the pet carrier was unbearable.

The whimpering, howling and barking continued nonstop. And, although the black cocker spaniel had not eaten a bite since the evening before, he had developed diarrhea and had completely covered his cage in a putrid dark fluid. The dog's long, black hair was wet with his own mess, compounding his misery. Any passing driver whose windows were down could hear the dog's cries of despair.

The voice from the front had gone from offering reassurances to singing before lapsing into long silences followed by loud, angry outbursts. When the smell of defecation filled the car – even with the windows down – the driver suddenly lost all self-control.

Tumbling out of the door, the driver managed to move around the front of the car and to the passenger side away from traffic. Looking toward the rear of the station wagon, where the dog continued his howling, the driver suddenly screamed, "Shut up, shut up, shut up! Why are you doing this to me? I am doing my best to take care of you!"

With that outburst the driver turned to look at the green field stretching away from the interstate. The land was flat, the soil fertile and the grass that grew would soon be cut and bailed for hay. The open view of land and sky struck the driver oddly, stirring emotions that couldn't be understood. The destination was near and although the driver had expected the South Carolina landscape to feel welcoming, depression seemed to be setting in. Looking again at the back of the station wagon, the driver knew the only way to continue was to get rid of the stench – and that meant getting rid of the dog.

CHAPTER THIRTY-SIX

When the three officers departed from the Larson's home, the Chief's first call was to Julia. She answered on the first ring. "Ms. Julia Frank, my favorite reporter!" Chief cooed, avoiding his typical pet names he usually used since he had another officer in the car with him.

"It's about time you called, Chief. I've got a life outside waiting for you."

"I know, I know, and you have the patience of Job," he teased. "How about meeting us at Java Junkies at Settlers Landing? It's close to the station and I'll want to check in on things."

"Sounds good, are you on your way now?"

"Yep. ETA is 15 minutes. See you then?"

"Yes, I'll be there. You have a photo of the dog?"

"As a matter of fact we do," he responded with an appreciate look over at Sergeant Walker.

With Julia set, the Chief turned his attention to Sergeant Walker. "So, what are you thinking?"

Sergeant Walker reflected for a moment and then looked at

the Chief. He had so much respect for this man and couldn't understand why the Chief seemed to have taken a liking to him. The last thing he wanted to do was let him down. It was worth all the teasing he took from the rest of the squad to be able to shadow the Chief and learn from him. "I think something's not quite right," he finally responded. "Something they aren't telling us. There's also something not right about the relationship with the dad and the computer being taken out of the house just this morning. It's not a coincidence."

Chief nodded appreciatively. "Yep. You know what it is – the missing piece that no one is telling us?"

"No, I don't. Do you?"

"I've got my suspicions, but it's too soon to say."

Sergeant Walker studied his notes as the Chief turned right off of Mercury Boulevard onto Pembroke. When the Chief's phone rang, the number told him it was the dispatcher's desk. He pushed the button for speaker phone, "Chief Johnson."

"Chief, it's Corporal Easley at the desk. Sir, I wanted to report to you that the auto taken by the Larson boy has been located on Ralph Street back at the end of the loop. No sign of the missing boy."

"Ralph Street... What is that close to...it's not ringing any bells."

"Sir, it's right off Buckroe, just a block down from St. Joseph's Catholic Church."

"Good work. I'm right around the corner so I'll drop Sergeant Walker off at the station and head over to St. Joseph's. There's a few folks there I need to talk to anyway."

Chief Johnson filled Sergeant in on the details as he turned onto Lincoln Street and a couple of minutes later pulled into the

157

station. He put the car in park and got out to wait for Officer Lacey to pull in behind. The Chief motioned for Sergeant Walker to join him for a quick update with Investigator Lacey.

"Lacey, I know you've always wanted some alone time with Julia and this is your chance. I need to head over to St. Joseph's. The car Kevin Larson was driving was found a block away from the Church. Sergeant Walker is going to stay here and get the APB out on Kevin." He looked over at Sergeant Walker. "Then I want you over in Fox Hill talking to neighbors. Where's the photo of the dog?"

Sergeant Walker handed the photo of Michael, Kevin and Calvin to the Chief who passed it to Investigator Lacey. "You take this and meet with Julia. Go ahead and tell her about Kevin but privileged, you hear. She is not to follow this one until we get the dog story done. I want it in every print and online news venue that will take it. ASAP. Everyone know what they've got to do?"

"Yes, sir," both men echoed as the Chief turned back to his car.

"Chop-chop!" he said, snapping his fingers loudly in the air before closing the car door behind him.

CHAPTER THIRTY-SEVEN

At 10:00 a.m., the watch on Father Patrick's watch began to beep. "Oh dear me," he said with disbelief. "Where has the time gone?"

"Are you saying mass this morning?" Bishop Grogan asked, embarrassed that he had taken so much of Father Patrick's time for his own needs.

"Yes, at 11:30. Not to worry, we still have plenty of time. I set my watch so I won't get carried away with other activities and forget," he said with a chuckle. "I sometimes do that at my age, you know."

Bishop Grogan smiled and nodded. "Yes, I know all too well. Do you mind if I join you?"

"I would be honored, Bishop, and the few who show up for mid-day Mass will be delighted." Father Patrick busied himself washing up the dishes and putting them away while Bishop Grogan excused himself to the bathroom where he stood for several minutes over the sink splashing cold water onto his face.

When the two men left the house and walked around the

corner to the front door of the church, only one car in addition to the Bishop's stood in the parking lot. "I believe that car belongs to the Church secretary, Sarah Pulley," Father Patrick explained seeing the direction of the Bishop's gaze.

"Very good. I've been wanting to meet her and today will be as good a day as any," he said, trying not to sound bitter toward one of the main complainants against Father Mario.

Though Father Patrick picked up the constraint in the Bishop's voice, he did not question. The two moved together up the brick steps and Father Patrick jingled the heavy key playfully as he shuffled ahead to open the large, wooden door for the Bishop. Finding the door unlocked, he looked back over his shoulder. "Aye, it looks like Mrs. Pulley's going to let us in today after all," he said cheerfully, stepping aside to allow the Bishop to pass.

Inside the church, the noise from the busy street outside became muted and both men noted the calm serenity that the small church offered. Bishop Grogan followed Father Patrick as he made his way toward the church offices to where Sarah Pulley's desk was stationed. She was speaking on the phone in hushed tones and quickly ended the conversation when she saw them approaching.

"Good morning, Mrs. Pulley, I'd like to introduce you to Bishop Grogan," Father Patrick began.

Sarah Pulley stood from behind her desk and welcomed the Bishop with some reservation. The letter she and the other parishioners had sent two months earlier remained unanswered and many of the parishioners had already begun growing impatient, even before yesterday's tragedy occurred. Little did she know that the Bishop's response, expressing his confidence in Father Mario's innocence following an obligatory investigation and requesting that the committee stop meeting, had been sent the previous morning to Allen Conner's home.

"I thought this would be a good time for us to chat," Bishop Grogan offered, working hard to conceal his previous judgments. "I hope I'm not disturbing your work."

"Not at all Bishop Grogan, I'll just put the phone on voice mail and then we won't be interrupted should the phone ring."

"That sounds fine, Sarah. Shall we go sit in the church?" he asked, knowing that Sarah would find that an odd place for such a personal topic of discussion. Over the years, the Bishop had learned that people found it easier to conceal the truth when tucked away in an office than they did sitting in the womb of the church with the eyes of Christ all around. He smiled at his own cleverness when he saw her hesitant acceptance of his offer.

"Do you require anything more of me Bishop?" asked Father Patrick, resuming his professional tone in place of the more intimate one they had shared for the better part of the morning.

"Not a thing Father, please go about your routine. We'll only be about half an hour and then I will be free to assist you with any preparations."

"Very well. I'll be in the sacristy should you need anything," Father Patrick said as the three of them moved toward the open double doors leading to the sanctuary. Once inside, all three dipped their fingers into the font of holy water placed at the entrance and crossed themselves in unison. For Sarah, the act was habitual; but for the two men of the Church, they were reminded of their initiation into their faith.

As Bishop Grogan led Sarah toward the front of the church, the water on his fingers left him asking for a prayer of protection. He wondered if this feeling was due to Sarah or something else. He rubbed his fingers gently together until the wetness vanished. Stepping aside, he held his hand toward the left of the church indicating Sarah to take a seat. *Three pews from the front should do it,* he thought as he slid into the pew next to her.

On the other side of the church, Bishop Grogan saw Father Patrick making his way to the sacristy, his jovial demeanor emanating from across the sanctuary. *How fortunate I am to have such a wonderful friend,* he thought. *Truly a gift!*

He turned back to Sarah who was shifting uncomfortably beside him. "Shall we begin with a prayer?" he asked as he reached to pull the kneeler forward.

"Yes, of course," Sarah answered. She'd never had a private consult with a Bishop before so she had no idea what to expect. The two figures knelt side by side and Bishop Grogan cast his eyes to the large wooden crucifix that hung behind the altar. "In the name of the Father, and of the Son and of the Holy Spirit," he began as they both crossed themselves.

"Amen," Sarah echoed quietly.

Just as Bishop Grogan took a deep breath to begin his prayer, a crashing noise was heard from the sacristy, followed by a moaning wail. Bishop Grogan jumped from the pew and ran across the church to the room off to the side of the altar where Father Patrick had entered just a moment before. The few seconds it took to reach the door of the sacristy seemed like minutes during which time the Bishop was filled with a wretched dread. He knew then that his prayer against evil was for whatever lay behind the door.

When he opened the door, he immediately saw Father Patrick on the floor, he appeared to have fallen backward and his head was propped against the sacrarium where the items used during Holy Communion were washed. Father Patrick held his right hand tight against his chest and his left hand was raised as if trying to rid himself of a horrid vision. Bishop Grogan ran quickly to his friend and knelt beside him. Father Patrick was saying something and Bishop Grogan leaned closer to hear.

"Terrible, terrible," he gasped. "Look at the vestments, I think he's dead."

Just as Bishop Grogan turned to look to the back of the room where the vestments hung, he heard Sarah's shrill scream. Dressed in his acolyte robe lay Kevin Larson, blue and stiff. Bishop Grogan gasped at the sight and was momentarily torn between the need to waken the boy from the dead and run away. He crossed himself and walked over to where the dead boy lay clutching a framed photo to his chest with one hand while holding an envelope in the other. Just as Bishop Grogan was reaching for the envelope, he heard another scream from Sarah.

"He's having a heart attack, Bishop!" she shouted.

Bishop Grogan looked back at his friend lying upon the floor. His face was ashen and both of his fists were clenched against his heart. "Call 9-1-1!" he shouted to Sarah, who stood in a state of shock. "Call 9-1-1!"

Sarah turned and groped at the door. She pulled it open and made her way out of the sacristy. Fear caught in her throat, a sob waiting to burst through. In her distress, she didn't even see Chief Carl Johnson enter the church and wave to her.

From inside the church, Chief Johnson heard an anguished voice calling out, "Patrick, stay with me! Patrick, it's okay. Everything will be okay!" The Chief ran as quickly as he could to the door from which the voice came. He saw Bishop Grogan leaning over Father Patrick who was clearly in cardiac arrest. The Chief rushed over and checked his vitals before beginning CPR. It wasn't until the emergency rescue arrived and took over that he turned around and saw Kevin Larson lying on the floor in a white robe.

"Hello Kevin, I'm sorry I got here too late," the Chief whispered. "Who do you have with you?" he asked, looking at the photo clutched in his arms. Reaching for a small linen laying on the table, he used it to lift to corner of the frame. It was an enlarged photo of him with Michael and the black cocker spaniel Calvin. He gently released the photo and turned to head for the car. He needed to radio the station and notify the coroner's office. It was going to be another tough day but at least this death would be easily solved.

Chief Johnson knew the boy had taken his own life and he knew with every bone in his body why. It would all be in the letter that the boy held in his hand, no doubt. The Chief had seen this pattern before and it never had a happy ending.

CHAPTER THIRTY-EIGHT

While Father Mario read from the file, Father Cameron returned to the window and gazed out at the back yard. A day didn't go by that he didn't want to pinch himself to make sure he wasn't dreaming. He felt so grateful for the life he had – a wonderful church community, a home with cook and housekeeper and the opportunity to help others. Behind him, his friend and brother in the Church had thought the same thing until just yesterday. How fleeting – or in Father Mario's case – how blind happiness can be.

"I know we've talked about this before," said Father Mario, "but do you think these threats are real or just some kind of sick joke?"

Father Cameron turned from the window and considered his friend for a moment. Yes, they had had many discussions over the threats that were received last summer both in the mail and in the collection plate. Father Cameron wondered if Father Mario was having second thoughts about their validity. Maybe he just needed to hear, once more, that his concern was legitimate. "At first I thought it might have been a joke, but I admit it got a little scary when they began appearing in the collection plate on Sundays."

"Yes, it frightened me too. What kind of person communicates in this way?"

"It's hard to say, really. I guess my biggest question is what outcome did the sender really hope to achieve?"

"I wonder. Strange, too, how they suddenly stopped. I guess that's why the Bishop chalked them up to a bad joke."

"Well, now that we have the opportunity to share with the police, they might have a better idea how to answer these questions. They might also know if other churches have received similar threats."

For a few minutes, neither man spoke – each lost in his own thoughts. Finally Father Mario placed the folder back on Father Cameron's desk, stood and stretched. "I guess we should give this file to the police. We really don't know if the Bishop kept the originals or not. Besides, if he did, they're probably locked up in Richmond."

"Yes, I agree. I expect we'll hear from the police soon. In the meantime, it's in the bottom left drawer at the back should you need it when I'm not here."

"Do you mind driving me over to Fox Hill? I need to get my car and then I'd like to go by the house and pick up some clothes since it appears I'll be staying with you until the Bishop tells me I can return..." His voice dropped as he considered how it would feel to go back to St. Joseph's with so much changed. One family dead, many of the members of the congregation against him. Perhaps he would never return.

When he contemplated what other options existed in his life, he felt even more depressed than before. What would he do? If he went back to Texas he could stay with his mother, but she would nag him until he confessed that he'd left the Church. He remembered when he first told her that he was going to become a Catholic priest – she became hysterical and kept telling him that he would go straight to hell. Suddenly the thought of going to Texas didn't seem like an option after all.

CHAPTER THIRTY-NINE

Newspaper reporter Julia Frank wasn't impressed when Investigator George Lacey showed up solo. She took the photo from him and studied it closely. "Who are the two boys? The one of the left looks like one of the Conner boys."

"Yes, the one on the left is Michael Conner, the oldest son of the family murdered yesterday. The one of the right is his best friend Kevin Larson."

"Oh, I'd like to talk to him," she said, suddenly interested.

"That might be hard to do right away," the investigator replied matter-of-factly. "He was reported missing this morning by his mother. They haven't seen him since early yesterday."

"Connection?" she asked, knowing he wouldn't tell her either way.

"Too soon to say," he replied, not elaborating.

Julia looked hard at Investigator Lacey, unimpressed. She saw a short, aging, spreading, balding, white man who just happened to be in uniform – a symbol of power, as if being a white man wasn't enough. She had to fight to keep her lips from curling in front of him. "Can I keep the photo?"

"Afraid not. We're gonna need it back at the station. Just a black cocker spaniel – Google it if you forget what he looks like," Investigator Lacey replied coolly. He wasn't dumb, even if people frequently judged him as slow. He could feel that she didn't like him and he could guess why. Some people just carried their ancestry around their necks like a badge. Julia Frank was another one of them and he could do without her. He didn't even like her style of writing and never read a word she wrote on account of it. She was just another newspaper starlet who would do anything to get ahead – they come a dime a dozen.

Julia reluctantly handed the photo back over and wished she'd been friendlier instead of letting her sentiments get the best of her. *Oh well, too late now,* she thought. Besides, she always had Chief Johnson.

CHAPTER FORTY

Fathers Cameron and Mario said little as they drove into the Fox Hill neighborhood. Every few minutes Father Mario would indicate which street Father Cameron should turn on, but otherwise they were quiet. When they turned onto Mimosa Crescent, Father Mario felt a throb in his heart and his pulse began to race. In the distance, they could see the yellow police tape across the front door swaying in the gentle summer breeze.

"You okay," Father Cameron asked, as he pulled up alongside Father Mario's car.

"Yes, I'm fine. Numb, but fine. Thanks for the ride. I guess I'll see you back at the ranch?"

Father Cameron wasn't sure the best way to respond. Bishop Grogan had given him specific instructions that Father Mario was not to leave the house until further notice and he was already breaking that promise. He didn't want his friend to feel like he was in trouble or that he didn't have the Bishop's trust and support; but, he needed to keep his word to the Bishop. "How about I follow you over to St. Joseph's? I hear Father Patrick

O'Brien is there to help you out until all this mess passes. I've liked him since we first heard him lecture in seminary. Do you mind?"

"Of course I don't mind. Go ahead, I'll be right behind you."

Father Cameron drove slowly forward and watched in his rear view mirror until he saw Father Mario's car pull away from the curb. During the fifteen minute drive to St. Joseph's they had been separated a couple of times due to traffic lights. Each time, Father Cameron had become apprehensive.

He felt a sense of responsibility for Father Mario, not only because he was under instructions from Bishop Grogan, but also because he considered Father Mario one of his best friends. Over the years, Father Mario had tended to be somewhat needy and Father Cameron was always the one who looked out for him.

When the two cars pulled into the parking lot at St. Joseph's, Police Chief Carl Johnson was standing there with his hands on his hips. The two priests had no sooner parked their cars than screaming sirens were heard coming in all directions. The two men got out of their cars and stood agape while police officers ran into the church, in the direction that the Chief pointed. Fathers Cameron and Mario exchanged a quick glance and then quickly made their way toward the door.

"Hold up!" Chief Johnson shouted, as he took long strides towards the two priests. "Not so fast." The two priests stopped and waited for Chief Johnson to offer some explanation.

"I'm afraid I can't let you go in right now," the Chief said, looking first at Father Mario and then to Father Cameron. "There's a body inside and the crime unit just arrived. We're still waiting on the coroner."

"What! A body?" babbled Father Mario, unbelieving.

"I'm afraid so. A young boy."

Father Mario felt his knees grow weak and he sat down on soft grass next to the sidewalk where the three men had been standing. "I just can't believe this, I just can't believe... Who is it?" he pleaded. "Please tell me who."

"I can't say. He hasn't been positively identified. He looks about 16, short brown hair."

"Oh God, no! No!" said Father Mario, dropping his face into his hands.

Chief Johnson watched the grieving priest closely, "Do you know who it is?" he asked curiously. When Father Mario did not respond the Chief knelt beside him and repeated sternly, "Do you know the name of the boy lying dead inside your church?"

"I have a bad feeling," Father Mario managed at last, shaking his head from side to side. "I've just got this bad feeling."

Chief Johnson stood up and turned back to Father Cameron. "I'll need the two of you to come down to the police station to answer some questions. I'm just waiting on someone from the coroner's office to show up and then I'll be able to leave. I suggest you drive Father Mario. He looks to be in a state of shock... again. I wouldn't want him driving in this condition."

"Yes, of course," Father Cameron responded. "Is Father Patrick here, by chance?"

"Father Patrick was taken to the hospital by ambulance just a couple of minutes before you arrived. He appears to have had a heart attack."

"Is he okay?" Father Cameron asked, clearly concerned.

"He was breathing, but it didn't look good," Chief Johnson

confided. "Ah, here's the coroner. Give me a few minutes and we'll go."

Father Cameron looked at Father Mario sitting on the grass, his face ghostly pale. Whatever evil was shadowing this church, it was merciless. He said a silent prayer of protection and crossed himself. Dropping to one knee he put his hand on his friend's shoulder. "I'm going to drive us to the police station. I've got the file from my desk in my brief case."

Father Mario nodded his consent without raising his eyes from the line of tiny dark ants marching across the sidewalk. He didn't see Sarah Pulley walking down the church steps with Chief Johnson and Sergeant Walker. They walked her over to a patrol car and helped her into the back seat. Sarah Pulley had not missed seeing Father Mario slumped over in the grass. Her eyes narrowed as she glared at him with contempt.

Sergeant Thomas Walker exchanged a quick word with Chief Johnson, glanced over at the two priests, then walked around to the driver's side and got in. As he drove past, Sarah Pulley continued to glare at Father Mario – who, of all those present, was the only one unaware of her hate being cast upon him.

"I can't go directly to the station," Chief Johnson said to Father Cameron from a few spaces down where he stood next to his police car. "But this would be a good time for the two of you to drop by the station for questioning. I've got a personal call I need to make and then I'll join you there. Know where you're going?"

Father Cameron nodded affirmatively and then reached his hand down to help Father Mario back to his feet. "We need to go now Steve. Let me help you up."

Father Mario reached numbly for Father Cameron's hand and the two priests ambled to Father Cameron's car to join the procession back to the Hampton police department.

CHAPTER FORTY-ONE

Bishop Grogan followed the ambulance as best he could though Chief Johnson had firmly told him to drive slowly and carefully. As he drove, he thought about how the chief had so confidently administered CPR to Father Patrick who, after clutching his chest in agony, had stopped breathing. The memory played in slow-motion, over and over: waiting for emergency services to show up; seeing the sweat drip from Chief Johnson's forehead, down his face and drop onto the man whose heart he was manually pumping; watching the rise and fall of Father Patrick's chest as the officer shared the oxygen from his own lungs; the feeling of utter helplessness as his eyes turned from the body of the dead boy to the body of his fallen friend.

When he arrived at the hospital, his initial inquiries were answered with, "Sorry, no family member has requested your services on behalf of the patient."

"But I am the closest thing to a family member he has!" the Bishop retorted. "His parents are long dead and he has no siblings. All of his extended family are back in Ireland. He's a priest in my diocese and I am the closest thing to kin you're going to find!"

"We'll have to check with the doctor on duty."

You do that, was what he wanted to say, but replied instead with a thank you that he hardly choked out before turning abruptly on his heel and scanning the halls for a place to sit.

He noticed, for the first time, the faces of others whose own emergencies had brought them in. A Hispanic family huddled together in one corner of the waiting area. The man wore a pair of jeans and a black button-up long-sleeved shirt with the sleeves rolled up to his elbow. He had his arm draped protectively over the shoulder of the woman that Bishop Grogan presumed to be his wife. She cried softly into a tissue, her long dark hair hanging around her face like a veil, while two small girls played at her feet.

In another part of the emergency room he saw an African American man in a wheel chair. He was obese, his legs as huge as tree trunks, and his ankles and feet so swollen that Bishop Grogan couldn't imagine the man could have ever walked. Diabetes does that to folks – all the more reason why Bishop Grogan supported healthcare reform with more focus on prevention rather than focusing only on treatment.

He had not brought his briefcase in from the car, as he knew there would be no way he could focus on work. Instead, he spent the rest of the morning and early afternoon alternating between pacing the floors, starring at the television mounted on the wall in the emergency waiting room and consoling those who saw his collar and – without consideration that he might be in fear of losing his own loved one – asked him for prayers of intervention and mercy for their own. After all, a man of the cloth must always serve the people, regardless of his own needs.

Once the emergency room staff understood the relationship between Bishop and Priest, his frequent trips to the nurses' desk provided the most important facts. Father Patrick was alive but in a coma and the staff indicated he would be moved to intensive care as soon as space became available. Repeated requests to see his friend – even as priest – were met with refusal.

That left Bishop Grogan with a lot of time to reflect on the last two days. He felt numb from it all, as if everything had spun out of control. He'd felt so sure of himself just yesterday, but now a knot of fear tightened in his stomach as he thought of the nameless boy lying in his acolyte's robe, lips blue from the kiss of death. *Dear God,* he thought, *I shall never get this memory from my mind. Another ghastly recollection to add to that of my brother. What's the point in all this pain?*

It was almost 3:00 p.m. when Dr. Wei Chu, senior staff cardiologist, approached Bishop Grogan. Dr. Chu made no pretenses about the severity and would offer no guarantee of survival, especially given that the patient was still in a coma. The Bishop struggled to understand Dr. Chu through his heavy accent, and had to ask him more than once to repeat himself.

What Bishop Grogan did understand from Dr. Chu was that Father Patrick was still not fully stabilized. It was not possible to determine the extent of damage to the brain or other organs from lack of oxygen; nor was it possible to determine the cause of the heart attack and make any immediate treatment recommendations other than stabilization.

When the conversation ended, Dr. Chu asked if he wanted to walk with the patient as they wheeled him up to intensive care.

Bishop Grogan nodded affirmatively and caught the lump forming in his throat. Suddenly, he felt afraid; not only for Father Patrick but for himself. Too many things hitting close to home. Too much too fast.

CHAPTER FORTY-TWO

Jenny Larson sat on the edge of Kevin's bed and closed her eyes. With her thoughts, she sought him out, called to him with her mind, screamed to him to hear her pleas... *Come home! Come home! Everything will be all right...* So deeply entrenched in her own world, she didn't hear the doorbell ring.

Outside the front door, Chief Johnson prepped himself like he had done so many times before on such dreadful occasions as this. He had not come directly over from the church, but instead had driven up Beach Road to State Park Drive and took a walk on the beach at the Grandview Natural Preserve.

He and Tanya had never had children but they had lots of nieces and nephews – a couple of them the same age as Kevin Larson. He tried to imagine how he would tell his brother and sister-in-law that their son was dead. He tried to imagine how it would feel to have had a son and lose him. He knew that he would never know the pain and never be able to truly empathize, no matter how much sympathy he might have in the matter. That made it all the harder to break the news to Jenny Larson.

Chief Johnson rang the bell a second time. The front door was open and he looked through the glass of the storm door for any sign of movement. Just as he was about to open the storm door and call into the house, he saw Caroline peek her head around the corner. She held one ear bud in her hand, the white wire coiled around and attached to the pink iPod in her opposite hand. She saw him through the glass and approached the door hesitantly.

"Hi, Caroline. Is your mom home?"

"Yes, I'll get her for you. Come in."

Chief Johnson stepped into the living room and took a deep breath as Caroline disappeared down the hallway calling after her mom. A second shout of, "Mom!" elicited a response from Jenny, who came out of Kevin's room to answer Caroline's call.

"That police chief is back. He's in the living room."

Jenny ran down the hall and into the living room where Chief Johnson stood just inside the door. When she greeted him, her face was drawn and her top lip had begun to twitch.

"Mrs. Larson, can we sit down?" he asked, more of a suggestion than a question.

Without speaking she turned and led him over to the two chairs where they had sat just a couple of hours earlier. She turned and looked at him, eyes glistening with tears waiting to fall. *She knows*, he thought. *Mothers always know.*

"We found your car on Ralph Street just a couple of blocks from the church." He paused before continuing. "And we found your son. I'm sorry..."

Jenny Larson gasped. The tears broke from the rims that had previously held them. "Where was he?"

"In the church. We were too late to save him. Sarah Pulley

identified him."

The Chief had come to learn that, when overcome by grief, humans make a sound that transcends barriers of race, ethnicity and language. It is a sound that comes from deep within the human soul – reaching out into the universe in a plea for understanding, for mercy, for time to stand still. In that moment, sitting in the living room of the Larson family, Chief Johnson heard the grieving moans again. He heard them from Jenny, who had fallen from her chair onto the floor; and he heard them from Caroline who stood against the wall of the hallway, iPod at her feet, her head raised in a wail of suffering.

Chief Johnson reached down in an attempt to comfort Jenny and try to right her into her chair but she refused to budge. He knelt down beside her and offered condolences and reminded her of Caroline who, by that time, had slid down the wall into a squat. Jenny raised her head and looked for her daughter. Unable to stand, she crawled on hands and knees until the two were joined in embrace.

The Chief gave the two women a few minutes before joining them. "Can I call your husband for you? It might be best if he came home to be with you two. I'm sure he would want to know."

Jenny snapped her head up and glared at him with a rage in her eyes. "He can rot in hell for all I care! This is his fault... his fault! Where is my son now? I have to see him. I have to be with him..."

"He's at the morgue. Once you have seen him, we'll need to determine the cause of death. An investigation will be necessary just to rule out any foul play, though it is not suspected."

Jenny closed her eyes and let her head drop. Caroline stared at Chief Johnson with hurt eyes as if he had brought all this upon them. "Just tell me what I need to do," Jenny said weakly. "Whatever I need to do."

The Chief didn't say anything for a moment and the three of them huddled together on the floor. Jenny continued to sob – long, deep moans that came from so deep within that Chief Johnson imagined the God of the Universe couldn't possibly ignore her pain. He shifted from his knees and stood slowly. He reached down a hand for each of the women in an effort to move them to a more comfortable place. Neither accepted his offer so he squatted again to be at face level with Jenny.

"Mrs. Larson, I need to understand why you said your husband is responsible for Kevin's death. I know this is a painful time for you, but that statement requires an explanation. Is there something more you need to tell me?"

Jenny threw her head back as if a great pain had just struck her. She brought her hands up and crossed them over her chest and let out another long moan that erupted into heaves as she momentarily fought for breath.

Chief tried again. "Mrs. Larson... Jenny, please. For Kevin's sake, is there anything more you need to tell me?"

Suddenly Caroline looked up, dark mascara smearing her young face, "I'll tell you," she said. "I'm not afraid of Dad," she said angrily, looking at her mother. Putting a hand protectively on her mother's arm she added, "Don't worry, Mom. It's easier this way." Then turning to Chief Johnson, she told him the family's dark secret.

CHAPTER FORTY-THREE

Julia Frank would do just about anything for a good story. And, although this notion of writing a missing dog story was, at first, the most whack thing she had entertained in a long while, it had started to grow on her. The Chief was right, people love dogs. Dogs and kids and bunnies... She let out a long sigh and looked at her GPS to get an updated estimate on her arrival. "Ten more minutes," she said out loud.

She pulled down the visor and slid the mirror open. Her lipstick was still fresh. *Maybe a little more gloss,* she thought. She reached over and prowled through her handbag with one hand, allowing her eyes to alternate between handbag and road. She'd gotten the name of Jack Mellon from one of the Cocker experts that the AKC had directed her to. Supposedly he was one of the best dog trainers around but had gotten out of the show ring claiming it was too political. It didn't matter to Julia. She just wanted the best there was to give her everything she needed to make this the best f'ing dog sob story of the century.

Her mind went back to the uncomfortable meeting with

Officer Lacey. Was their dislike for each other always mutual or did she set the tone from the moment he walked in and she gave him "the look." *Just what I wanted to see – another fat, white, balding, honkie.* Just as quickly as she realized her fault, she forgave herself. *No need to blame myself,* she thought. So, if this Jack man turns out to be another George Lacey I *swear* I'll be sweet as momma's apple pie.

Julia turned her Honda Accord off 264 and onto the Virginia Beach Expressway. She slowed to check the street signs until she saw Baltic. She swung a left and counted three blocks until she saw 24th street. Three blocks from the beach, she wondered what a house would cost. In this section of town, the houses were smaller, but well kept.

She slowed even further and began reading off the house numbers until she found 444. Parallel lines painted onto the streets indicated parking spaces and she pulled in to the first one, right in front of the small, white house. She put the car in park, surveyed the front porch for any signs and life and turned off the car. Grabbing her notebook and portable Canon, she opened the door and was greeted by raucous rounds of barking from within the screened-in porch. *And this is why I'm not a dog person,* she thought sourly as she shut the car door and made her way to the sidewalk that lead to the house. Just as she approached the door of the porch, a lean man with long, blond hair pulled back in a pony tail came out of the house and onto the porch to shush the dogs. He saw the red Honda at the curb and turned to see Julia standing at the door.

"Hi, you must be the newspaper reporter."

"Julia. And you must be the cocker-beast trainer."

"Jack," he said with a laugh. He walked over to unlock the screen door to invite her in.

"Do they bite?" she asked with obvious apprehension.

"Don't be silly; these are love bugs. They might lick you to death but they won't bite. Promise."

"Sorry, but I can't handle licks either. Did I mention on the phone that I'm not really a dog person? This meeting is just to give me enough exposure to the dogs so that I can write with a reasonable amount of authority."

"I see. Well, you aren't going to be able to do that if you stand out there all day so you might as well prepare yourself and step on in. We can sit right here on the porch and I'll tell you everything I know."

Remember the end goal, she told herself as she stepped into the doggie palace. On the right-side of the porch she saw two vinyl arm chairs that were too small for an adult. At first she thought that maybe Jack had young children but then when he whistled softly through his teeth and snapped his fingers, the dogs turned and jumped into an armchair. They made several circles in their respective chairs until finally each one dropped into the seat with a loud plop and turned to gaze curiously at her. Even Julia couldn't repress a smile as their tongues dropped out of their mouth and they panted, eyes closed, to ward off the heat of the day.

"See, they're not so bad now are they?" Jack asked teasingly.

"No, so long as they are over there and not on me, I guess they're okay." She looked around for a place to put her notebook and handbag so that she could snap a quick photo.

"How about over here," Jack suggested, reading her

thoughts. He motioned her to the other side of the porch where a wooden porch swing hung from the ceiling. On the side of the porch attached to the house was a small wooden table that held a coffee cup. Jack picked it up, suddenly self-conscious that the coffee left in the bottom had dried and caked nastily on the side. "Must have forgotten this one," he said smiling. "Go ahead and snap a few photos if you like and I'll be right back."

"You're not going to leave me by myself with these dogs are you?" she asked, suddenly panicked.

"Yes. Trust me. You'll be safe."

As Jack headed back into the house through the open door, Julia turned to watch the two dogs, hoping they still had their eyes closed. Only the lighter colored one still watched her and Julia believed her to be studying her for any apparent weakness. "Okay, so I'm afraid of dogs. Not everyone in the world loves you hairy beasts, you know." *Making small talk with dogs, what has gotten into me?* She set her things on the table and pressed the button on her Canon. The camera made a musical sound as the lens cap opened and two dog heads popped up and to looked at her quizzically.

For a moment she was afraid they'd jump out of their chairs and come for her; fortunately, Jack came out of the door behind her and the dogs' attention was suddenly diverted to see nothing but him. He carried two bottled waters and placed one on the table next to her things.

"Swing okay?" he asked casually, already walking over to take a seat. Julia had observed that the swing was the only place to accommodate two-legged occupants.

"Sure," she said, suddenly wondering if this dude was going

to try to hit on her. She hated it when white men hit on her. She focused instead on the dogs and snapped a few shots while they gazed lovingly at Jack.

"Is that a Canon?"

"Yeah. Powershot SD960. Love it."

"It's pink."

"It comes in boy colors too, if you're looking to buy one," she offered as she shifted position to take a few more photos of the dogs. A few shots later she turned the camera on Jack and snapped a few times more. She shut the camera off and placed it on the table and picked up her notebook and the bottle of water. "Thanks for the water. It's gonna be another warm one."

"Yeah, but I love it. Guess that's why I live on the beach. The kids like it too."

"How old are your kids," she asked, continuing the small talk.

"Well, the black cocker, his name is Austin, he's four. The blonde's name is Sugar and she's three."

Julia laughed. "You call your dogs kids? I thought you were talking about children."

"Nope, these are the only kids I have," he said smiling. "Do you want to see something really precious?"

"Sure," she said cautiously, still not certain how to read him.

"Follow me." Jake jumped up from the swing, placed his water bottle on the table and headed into the house. Julia followed him but stopped just inside the door.

"What exactly are you going to show me?" She wasn't feeling good about this.

He turned and saw her frozen in the door. "Come on, it's just right here on the other side of the bar." The kitchen was small and a island jutted out from the back wall creating a breakfast bar. Jack stood on the other side of the breakfast bar next to the kitchen table. He was looking down at the floor, a smile plastered all over his face. "Here, look."

Julia walked over to the bar and looked around the corner to see a 3x3 cardboard box, with the sides cut down to about six inches from the floor. Inside were seven black and blond puppies. Julia walked closer and dropped slowly to her knees.

"Go ahead, pick one up. I thought we'd better start slow – can't think of a better place to start than with a puppy."

Julia reached over and stroked the little, sleeping heads which suddenly began rooting around for milk. "How old are they?"

"Just three weeks. Precious aren't they?"

Julia looked back down at the litter, picked up one of the blonds and nestled it gently to her. Instinctively, she buried her nose into its soft fur. "Yes, this is probably the best place to start," Julia said, finally giving Jack a genuine smile. "I want to know everything there is to know about these dogs so don't leave anything out."

CHAPTER FORTY-FOUR

At the Hampton Police Station things were hopping. Sergeant Walker put Sarah Pulley in one interview room and asked Investigator Lacey, who had returned from his meeting with Julia, to take her statement about the morning incident in the church. By the time he had arranged that, Fathers Cameron and Mario were walking into the station, both ashen faced. Sergeant Walker explained that he would need to take separate interviews from them and asked Father Cameron to wait in the lobby while he interviewed Father Mario.

On the way to the interview room, Sergeant Walker swung by the break room and asked Father Mario if he'd like something to drink. There was a soda machine and a coffee pot as well as a vending machine full of candy bars and chips. Father Mario's throat suddenly felt tight and dry and he asked for water.

Sergeant Walker dropped coins into the machine and pressed a button and then repeated the procedure before pulling out two water bottles. He handed one to Father Mario and then showed him the way to the interview room.

Sergeant Walker had been curious about Father Mario and, although it was tragic what had happened this morning in the church, he was glad to have the opportunity to conduct the interview. Both men sat across from each other at a small, metal desk. Sergeant Walker crossed his legs and placed his writing pad on his knee and took a deep breath. Across from him, Father Mario appeared anxious, his lips pressed tightly together and his eyes alert. For a moment, the two men just looked at each other.

"Are you okay with my recording our interview?" Sergeant Walker asked.

"Yes, of course. Whatever you need to do."

Sergeant Walker pressed the button on the small recording device, took a deep breath and centered his focus on the man across from him. They began with the easy stuff: where he was from, where he went to school, what led him to became a priest.

Both men were eager to talk about the perceived threats against the Church – information that Chief Johnson had picked up from Father Mario on the ambulance ride to the hospital. Sergeant Walker was anxious because the Chief had been so curious to learn more. Father Mario was anxious because the file had been an albatross around his neck for almost two years. When Sergeant Walker asked why he thought the Church had been threatened, Father Mario opened the unmarked file that Father Cameron had given him in the lobby.

"About two years ago, I came home to find this taped to my door," Father Mario said, handing the first piece of paper across the table. "Well, not this one exactly – this is a copy. We turned all the originals over to Bishop Grogan when we met with him to discuss our concerns."

"Who is *we*?" Sergeant Walker asked.

"Father Cameron and me. I knew Father Cameron from seminary where we first became friends. I went to him first with my concerns just to see if he thought they were legitimate."

"And did he?"

"Not so much as first. During my first year here, I found three notes like this one on my door. A couple came through the mail from different states – Wyoming, Kansas. Then, they began showing up in the collection plate about a year ago. That's when Father Cameron became concerned and we decided to go to Bishop Grogan."

Sergeant Walker took each of the pages as Father Mario passed them over. Each page had only one line of text, cut from a variety of media, spelling out taunts and threats, not only against the Catholic Church, but to Father Mario personally.

YOU CATHOLICS ARE HELL BOUND. THAT MEANS YOU TOO!

YOU WILL ALL DIE.

PLAYING WITH LITTLE BOYS IS EVIL. YOU WILL GO TO HELL!

WHEN WILL YOU GET RELIGION?

GOD WILL PUNISH YOU!

"Are these in the order you received them?" Sergeant Walker asked.

"I think so as best I can remember. I penciled the dates received on the back of the originals but when Father Cameron copied them he didn't think to transcribe them."

DEATH WILL BECOME YOU ALL.

THE AVENGING ANGEL IS GOD SENT!

"When was the last letter received?"

"Last summer. Then they just seemed to stop."

"What was Bishop Grogan's take on the letters?"

"He said the church gets stuff like this all the time, often-times indicating exactly where they came from. Mostly from members in other churches who view the Catholic Church as evil. He judged the letters to be something an over-zealous teenager might do as a prank."

"What did you and Father Cameron believe?"

"We had no idea that the Church was known to receive threats like this. It's not the kind of stuff we learned in seminary. Father Cameron had never received anything like this although his house had been egged on Halloween. But nothing like this. We tried to respect Bishop Grogan's perspective; Father Cameron seemed to accept it with little difficulty but I never could. Something just felt... I don't know how to explain it... threatening to me."

Sergeant Walker made a note on his writing pad and leaned forward for emphasis. "Why were you at the Conner's home yesterday morning?"

Father Mario shook his head slowly, a far away look in his eyes. "I couldn't believe it was true. I thought that if I drove to their home, I'd find everything as it should be."

"And how should it have been, Father Mario?"

Father Mario shrugged his shoulders. "Not dead."

Did you know that Allen Conner was leading a committee to have you ousted as the parish priest? Sergeant Walker asked.

Father Mario sighed deeply. He was still beyond believing that his own community would have turned against him. "Bishop

Grogan informed me of the committee last night. I'm beside myself with disbelief."

"Is it possible that you knew about it before yesterday and that you went to the Conner's home to confront them?"

"Absolutely not!" Father Mario almost shouted. "I loved that family. I love them still," he added, his frame suddenly slumping into his chair. "They just didn't understand."

"Understand what?" Sergeant Walker pressed.

Father Mario was at the junction between civil and church law. Between stating what he did know and breaking the vows he had made in the Church. He looked sadly at Sergeant Walker. "They didn't understand the confidentiality between a priest and his confessors."

The two men sat in silence. Father Mario's gaze dropped to the table while Sergeant Walker continued his observations of the priest. When Sergeant Walker stood, he motioned toward the threatening papers spread out on the table. "We'll need to keep these. That's all for now Father Mario. Do you mind waiting in the lobby while I talk to Father Cameron?"

"Of course," Father Mario said, also standing. "Maybe I'll have a walk outside and stretch my legs."

As the two men entered the lobby, Father Cameron wasn't to be found. "I seemed to have lost a priest," Sergeant Walker said to the dispatcher on duty.

"Chief Johnson has him."

"Why don't you have a seat here? It may not be so long as I thought. Can I get you anything?"

"No thanks, I'm good."

Sergeant Walker went back to the interview room and

collected the pages, careful to keep them in the same order as Father Mario had them, and placed them in the folder. He knew the Chief would like to have a look at them with Father Cameron. He tapped the door of the interview room next to his and heard the Chief's voice beckon him in.

"You may want to have a look at this," Sergeant Walker said, handing the file to Chief Johnson. "I've finished up with Father Mario. Do you want to talk to him, too?"

"Yes, as soon as I finish up here. Maybe 20 minutes more."

"Yes, sir. I'll let him know."

Sergeant Walker closed the door behind him and headed back toward the lobby to give Father Mario an update. He scanned the lobby but saw no signs of the priest.

"It seems I've lost another priest," he said to the dispatcher, almost smiling.

"Oh that one? He just walked out a couple of minutes ago. We weren't supposed to hold him were we?"

"No. Nothing to hold him on. Let's just hope he comes back."

CHAPTER FORTY-FIVE

Bishop Grogan sat next to Father Patrick's bed in the intensive care unit. Although visitation was limited to ten minutes for family members, the Bishop had managed to persuade Dr. Chu to allow him to stay by Father Patrick's side. After the Bishop explained the sacrament of anointing the sick, the doctor had bowed his head slightly in understanding and said, "I have seen and experienced many great things through prayer."

The room where he sat was partitioned into three spaces separated by curtains that were drawn around each occupant's bed. Father Patrick was connected to a variety of machines that alerted the nursing staff to his heart rate, blood pressure, respiration and the speed at which the clear fluid was being injected into his blood stream through an IV in the crook of his right arm.

He looked closely at the face of his long time friend, remembering the many years that had passed since their first meeting in seminary. He could not remember a time when Father Patrick was not jovial, not a time when his face wasn't illuminated with a smile.

Now for the first time, Bishop Grogan saw the heavy lines in Father Patrick's face, the corners of his mouth turned down and the lids of his eyes bluish as if bruised. From the outside corners of his eyes ran a moist trail to his ears where they caught on the top of the lobe and then trailed downward into his ear. The Bishop wondered if, in fact, Father Patrick was crying and if so, were his tears a reflection of joy or of pain.

Bishop Grogan reached into his pant pocket and pulled out a small, black leather pouch cinched tightly at the top with a black leather cord. He pulled at the opening until the round, gold-plated tube engraved with the initials AG was visible. This small container held the sacred oil for anointing the sick and the Bishop carried it with him at all times. He placed the container on the nearby table and removed the lid.

Turning back to Father Patrick, he placed his hands the man's head, focused his mind and called forth to the heavens. Then, dipping his middle right finger into the oil, he made the sign of the cross on Father Patrick's forehead. "Through this holy anointing, may the Lord in his mercy help you with the grace of the Holy Spirit." Taking Father Patrick's hands, he again dipped his finger into the container and made the sign of the cross. "May the Lord, who frees you from sin, save you and raise you up. Amen."

He stayed in prayer posture throughout the afternoon and into the evening, without food or drink. He was fasting in honor of his friend. He was doing all that he knew to do as priest and minister, to be in the spiritual presence of God on behalf of his friend. The Bishop's eyes were closed in deep meditation, only his fingers moving gently over the ruby beads of his rosary when he heard Father Patrick try to speak. Startled, Bishop Grogan jumped quickly from the chair, leaned over the bed and gently touched Father Patrick's hand.

"Patrick, my friend! You have decided to stay amongst the living!" Bishop Grogan exclaimed in a loud whisper, the greatest smile upon his face. He looked warmly at his friend who had managed, in spite of his condition, to turn the corners of his drawn mouth ever so slightly upward. Father Patrick coughed a couple of times and his dry lips parted in an attempt to speak. Bishop Grogan leaned down closer to hear.

"I've seen him," he managed to say in a rasping voice.

"Seen who," the Bishop asked gently, thinking perhaps Father Patrick had seen the face of God.

"The boy. I've seen Kevin at the river."

The Bishop thought Father Patrick was hallucinating and reassured his friend as best he could.

"My friend, you've been in a coma. We didn't know if you would make it. Let me get the doctor."

"No, wait," Father Patrick struggled to raise his arm to reach for the Bishop but it only collapsed back on the bed.

Bishop Grogan took his hand and leaned in again. "What is it, my friend?"

"I must... go back... show him the way. He's afraid to cross... he sees them all waiting on the other side, beckoning him over..." Father Patrick's eyes opened slightly and then closed again, two fresh salty streams trailing out from the corners. He coughed a couple times more and began again. "I tried to tell him... there is a boat hidden in the reeds, just beyond his sight. He couldn't hear me. I've got to go back and reach him, to show him how to cross. He wants to get to the other side... but he doesn't know how... they are all waiting, singing joyfully... friends, grandparents, angels all calling him home. It's okay. It's all okay. Let's go home."

Bishop Grogan reassured his friend, "Yes, it is all okay. But won't you stay with us Patrick? Are you sure you can't stay longer?"

"Must go now... Kevin is waiting... Ah, you're happy to see me, are you laddie?" Patrick's voice faded as he gasped for breath and went through the motions of a cough, but nothing could be heard.

Bishop Grogan leaned in closer and held one of Father Patrick's cold hands.

"Yes, see here laddie..." Father Patrick's voice whispered so softly that Bishop Grogan's ear was turned inches in front of Father Patrick's mouth. "Here is the boat Kevin, let's cross together... they're all waiting... for you..."

Bishop Grogan had sat at the bed of many dying and had seen many things. He knew that his friend was choosing death over life. Though he hoped Father Patrick would stay in the world of the living, he now realized that Father Patrick was choosing his own fate. "In the name of God, and of the Father, and of the Son and the Holy Spirit," he whispered, crossing himself slowly.

Suddenly, the room was ringing with alarms. Bishop Grogan was quickly pushed aside by three members of the medical staff. He moved to the end of the bed and raised his hands in prayer, while the hands of the intensive care staff worked to resuscitate the dying man.

Bishop Grogan closed his eyes and repeated a commendation for his friend. "We have passed from death to life because we love each other. We have passed from death to life because we love each other..."

He imagined Father Patrick and Kevin in the boat, smiles upon their faces as they rowed eagerly away from the shore and across the water from this world to the next. *From all that is known, to all that is unknown.*

CHAPTER FORTY-SIX

Julia had everything she needed. After an awkward start, she and Jack, dog trainer extraordinaire, had finally connected and she felt confident that her story was ready to be told. She'd done all her homework. She'd made call after call. She'd even gone around the Conners' neighborhood asking any neighbor who would talk to her about the dog and its owners. She was ready.

She waved at Jack as she pulled away and followed the directions he'd given her to the nearest Starbucks. Make a left at the stop sign onto Arctic, second right onto 25th Street, left onto Pacific, right at Laskin. Easy. Left, right, left, right. Starbucks on the right. He'd suggested she work on her story on the beach, but Julia couldn't wait to get out of the heat and into air conditioning. She couldn't believe that Jack refused to turn the air conditioning on.

She wove her way to the oceanfront and parked in a paid lot just a block from the Starbucks. She was a sweaty mess and if she weren't so anxious to get the story out, she'd have gone straight home and showered first. She grabbed the soft-sided canvas bag from the passenger floorboard that held her MacBook. She stuffed her notebook and handbag into the canvas, double-checked that she had her ear buds.

The Starbucks line wasn't too bad and within 10 minutes she had secured a table on street side and was set up, with a tall ice cappuccino next to her. Although the story was bursting to come out, she could never predict how long it would take to get it just right. She booted up, opened Pandora and clicked on her Rihanna station. Ear buds in place, she heard the beat of the music begin. She loved to let the music jump-start her artistic flow. Seconds later, Rihanna was singing about pictures on the wall. Julia closed her eyes, let the rhythm take her and in moments the story opened itself up.

Two hours later, she sent her editor a text.

Just sent 2morrows front page. Ur gonna luv it.

No, this wasn't her usual newsworthy story. In fact, she'd never written anything quite like it -- but somehow it felt right. She was pleased, but with all of her big stories she never really knew how the reader would view it. That was the funny thing about writing – you just never knew. Five minutes later, her editor texted her back.

Great story Julia! I'm posting it online in 10 and sending it out over wire for anyone who will pick it up.

Her heart sunk. Online versions were good and she was pleased he was releasing it via wire, but what about print? There's nothing like seeing a feature story in print.

Then a second text came through.

This will be a sensation in print tomorrow. Good work!
Take rest of day off. :-)

She smiled to herself, closed her laptop and started to pack up. And to think, all this in two days and just one ice cappuccino. She reached over her shoulder as she got up and gave herself a pat. *Damn girl, this is getting too easy!*

CHAPTER FORTY-SEVEN

When Chief Johnson and Father Cameron came out of the interview room and into the lobby, Sergeant Walker was pacing in front of the door.

"Where's Father Mario?" the Chief asked, already sensing something not quite right.

"I don't know sir. He seems to have left the building."

Chief Johnson remained calm and appeared unconcerned. "Did you go out and look for him? Maybe he walked down to the water front to get some air."

"Yes, sir. I took a quick walk down and back and checked the coffee shops in the area but didn't see him."

"Did he know I was going to interview him after Father Cameron?"

"No, sir. He was already gone when I came back to tell him."

Suddenly the office was quiet as the hustle and bustle of work slowed enough to listen to the conversation. It seemed like the Chief's number one had screwed up. Around the office, glances were exchanged – none of which escaped either the Chief or Sergeant Walker. Chief Johnson took a slow spin around the room and just as quickly as the room had quieted, it came back to life.

"War room in five," he shouted, an indication that everyone on staff was to gather to discuss where things stood with the latest big case. Turning back to Father Cameron he added, "I hope you don't mind sticking around until Father Mario returns. When he does, would you ask him to wait, if it's not too inconvenient?"

"Yes, of course," Father Cameron answered, wondering what was going on. Not that he thought Father Mario capable of any wrong-doing, but it did seem strange that he would have just *disappeared*. "How long has he been gone?" he asked, turning to Sergeant Walker.

"About 40 minutes."

"That's nothing," said the Chief, smiling. "When it's 40 hours, we'll get concerned. War room," he added, looking directly at Sergeant Walker, and the two were off, leaving Father Cameron to wait and wonder.

In the war room, Chief Johnson looked around and saw most of the faces from the 0700 briefing. It was now 1600 hours and plenty had happened in the last nine hours – at least in his world. He pulled the board from this morning's briefing to the center of the room, picked up a red marker and drew a line down the middle of the board. "On the left side of the board is where we were this morning – not very far. On the right side of the board is where I want to see your progress. Who wants to start?"

"Still no black cockers at any of the animal shelters. I've even checked all the private rescues in the area – nothing to report,"

Zach offered to get things started. "We did find several photos of a black cocker spaniel and, I remember you said to give Ms. Julia Frank anything about the dog so I called to let her know I had them. She suggested I scan and email them to save her a trip – said she was out of town or something. So, she should have what she needs to get that dog story out tomorrow."

George Lacey and the Chief exchanged a look and Lacey shrugged. Julia hadn't said anything to him about having another source for a dog photo. *Well, good for her,* he thought sarcastically.

"While you were in the neighborhood, any leads on the cleaning lady?" the Chief asked, looking around the room.

"All we got on the cleaning lady was that she had been coming for the last two or three months," offered Lieutenant Eaton. "Older lady, short-cropped, silver hair, small-framed. No idea where she came from. Didn't ever arrive in a car. She always came with Mrs. Conner or showed up on foot."

"Thanks, Eaton. Weren't you also tracking the phones?"

"Yes, sir. Nothing to report."

"Nothing to report on gun registration either," Sergeant Walker added.

"Well, let's think about what we *do* have," said the Chief, feeling frustrated.

"Sarah Pulley says the priest did it," said Lacey, trying to ease the tension. "Of course, she doesn't have the first piece of evidence, but claims she knows he killed them all." He chuckled and shook his head.

"Which priest?" several voices asked.

"I don't think either of the priests have anything to do with the murders," Chief Johnson interjected. "We still abide by innocent until proven guilty – or at least have reasonable proof to put them under arrest," he reminded them.

In the back corner, the fax machine began humming. George Lacey walked over and looked at the first sheet coming through. "Looks like a prelim from forensics."

"What do they have?" the Chief asked.

"Nice," the investigator cooed, before looking up to a room of curious faces. "You're gonna love this, Chief. They've got DNA that doesn't match any of the family. Came from a tissue they collected out of one of the children's rooms. Nasal fluid."

Chief Johnson smiled, "That is a beautiful thing – a killer who gets all sentimental, blows their nose and doesn't think about the evidence. Which of the children's room?"

"Michael. The friend of the Larson boy."

"Interesting. Anything else?"

"The synthetic hair they found is the same material used in the majority of wig and toupee manufacturers." Lacey looked back to Eaton, "Did you guys find any wigs or toupees as you were looking through things?"

"Nope. Not a thing."

"Ah, there's more," offered Lacey. "The synthetic hair was short and silver." Excitement reverberated around the room.

"This is good," the Chief said. "We need to focus on the cleaning lady. Did we get any more names from Sarah Pulley?"

"During our interview she recalled a few names of folks who were missing from yesterday's meeting or left early," Lacey answered, "but she said she needed to check her list, which was in the file at work. I dropped her off at St. Joseph's where her car was parked but I didn't think to ask her to go in and get the

206

names. My bad."

"Your bad!" came a chorus of voices around the room, followed by laughter. "This is a murder case, not a walk in the parking lot," another voice called out.

"Walk in the park, you idiot," came a retort from the back.

"Enough already," Chief Johnson said. "Get it tomorrow and make sure you talk to anyone that we didn't interview yesterday," he said to Lacey. Then to the whole team he made it clear, "We've got to find this cleaning woman."

"Yes, sir," echoed across the room.

"By the way," the Chief asked, suddenly curious. "Any leads on the missing dog shit?" Laughter filled the room.

"As a matter of fact," said Zach, "We found a shit-load of dog shit in the outside garbage. I guess they had cleaned the yard that day. Really weird, though, whoever picked it up was very careful to triple-bag it and tie it nicely before tossing it in."

"Hmmm." Chief Johnson managed through a deep sigh as he folded his arms. "Was the dog a barker?"

"According to the neighbors the dog barked at everything, even his own family," offered Lieutenant Eaton.

"So what does that tell us?" the Chief asked, probing.

"That the perp was already in the house," came a response.

"That the perp could have been in the house and given the dog something to make it sleep and come back later," offered another.

"What else?" the Chief asked, pushing them to think harder.

"That the perp took the dog before evening and came back."

"The dog was already missing."

"Good," said Chief Johnson. "Now, which of these possibilities is most viable, given all we know?"

"That the perp was either already in the house or the dog was already missing," came the response after a long pause.

Chief Johnson nodded his agreement. "That's my thinking too, but we can't dismiss all the possibilities at this time." Through the windows of the war room the Chief saw the dispatcher mouthing the words, "Priest is back." He waved his understanding and dismissed his team. "Until 0700."

In the lobby, Fathers Cameron and Mario sat in the vinyl chairs in front of the dispatcher's desk. Father Cameron was speaking quietly into a phone and Father Mario was staring at the floor. "Nice walk?" the Chief asked cheerfully as he approached.

"Yes, it was," Father Mario answered, standing as the Chief approached. "Apologies for keeping you waiting. It's really lovely down at Settler's Landing. I've never spent much time down there."

Chief Johnson smiled again and nodded. "So glad you like the area. I know you spoke to Sergeant Walker earlier today so I hope you don't mind staying just a bit longer."

Father Mario smiled a sad smile. "Of course not," he said.

Father Cameron put his phone away and looked at Chief Johnson. "That was Bishop Grogan. Father Patrick passed away a few moments ago."

"I'm very sorry to hear that," the Chief offered sincerely. "I know this is a difficult time for all of you."

"Thank you," Father Cameron replied. "By the way, the Bishop said he was on his way down. He's hoping you'll be able to conduct your interview with him this evening as he wants to have Father Patrick's body transported back to Richmond as soon as possible and begin plans for the funeral."

"Yes, that would be fine," the Chief answered. *It's gonna be another long night. I hope my baby still loves me when I get home.*

CHAPTER FORTY-EIGHT

Bishop Grogan felt as though he had aged ten years in the last two days. He'd not slept well last night given the difficulty of the conversation he'd had with Father Mario. After tossing and turning most of the night, he had finally given up sleep altogether and contented himself to read the night away. He'd spent a wonderful morning with Father Patrick, for which he was grateful beyond expression. He'd fasted the entire day in prayer and was now on his way to the police station to answer questions about God only knows what. He was simply too tired to think about it.

He found a place to park near the police station and walked into the lobby to find Father Cameron napping in a chair. He sat down quietly next to the sleeping priest and thought that a nap seemed just the thing. No sooner had he sat down and closed his eyes than Chief Johnson was waking him with a gently shake of the shoulder.

"Nice nap?" he asked.

"Did I nap?" the Bishop asked, feeling momentarily confused.

"About 15 minutes," offered the dispatcher, who was sitting across from them.

"My goodness, I felt like I'd just sat down. Well, then," he said, standing. "Shall we?" he asked Chief Johnson.

"This way," the Chief extended his hand in the direction of the interview room.

"Oh, Father Cameron, I hope you don't mind that I'll be staying again this evening. I'll be over as soon as I'm finished here." Father Cameron nodded and replied, but the Bishop didn't hear him.

"I'm sorry to hear about Father Patrick," Chief Johnson began, once they'd settled into their chairs at the desk.

"Thank you for all you did to try to save him," Bishop Grogan replied, all his anger at the Chief from the day before now gone. "It was his time. I think he chose to go."

"What do you mean?" Chief Johnson asked, carrying on with the small talk, before getting to the more challenging questions.

"He came out of his coma long enough to tell me he was going back. He said he had to help a boy named Kevin across the river." Bishop Grogan shook his head sadly at the memory.

"Did Father Patrick know the dead boy?" the Chief asked, suddenly interested.

"What?" Bishop Grogan asked, confused.

"Kevin Larson, the dead boy that Father Patrick found in the church. Did he know him?"

Suddenly Bishop Grogan understood. He had not known that Kevin was the name of the boy who lay dead in the church, but now it all made sense. He felt a chill go through him, not of fright, but of the power of the world beyond his knowing. "No,

I'm certain he didn't know him. I think he just met him today...
at the river," the Bishop's voice sounded melodic, thoughtful.

"At the river?"

"Yes, Father Patrick said that Kevin couldn't cross the river.
He couldn't see the boat in the reeds and although Father Patrick
was trying to tell him where the boat was, Kevin couldn't hear
him. He said he had to go back and show Kevin the way over."

"I know this has been a long day for you, Bishop. It's been a
long day for all of us. But after we finish up here, I know there is
someone who would really want to hear this story."

"Who?"

"Kevin's mother. I think it would mean a lot. Would you be
willing to share with her?"

"Yes, of course. It will be a blessing to do so."

"In that case, let's be quick about the rest of it. Really, I just
have one question for you. Why didn't you take the threats that
Father Mario received seriously?"

Bishop Grogan took a deep breath. His voice sad, he told
Chief Johnson story after story of threats received by the Church.
Most of the stories he recounted came from what appeared to be
religious bigots whose holier than thou beliefs made them
intolerant to any other religious practices. The Bishop went on to
list many examples of religious bigotry just to make his point. It
was bullying on the grounds of religion, to be sure, the Chief
thought, as he listened. He had always known that
discrimination went much broader than gender and race.

"The Vatican used to track this kind of thing, but it was
simply too much to keep up with. In most cases, the threats were
just verbal. Most outright attacks against Catholics occur in areas

where there is civil unrest – India, Turkey, Venezuela, Kenya. That's not to say that there haven't been incidents in the US because there have been, but few and far between.

"The Church is in a tough position in that we don't want to accuse other religious faiths of attack. After all, we don't always know where the animosity is coming from – though we do have some thoughts on the subject. Most of all, we don't want to bring more negative press on ourselves. I don't need to tell you that we've had a good bit of it lately."

"Okay, I said only one question, but I really have to ask one more," said the Chief. "Why didn't you act on the accusation against Father Mario presented by members of his parish? Don't you think your inaction perpetuates the perception that you – the Catholic Church – are just covering up? That you're hiding a terrible secret?"

Bishop Grogan nodded his head in understanding. "Yes, I guess it does look that way sometimes. Maybe we're mistaken in not doing a better job communicating our processes for internal investigations and corrective actions. But I did conduct an investigation around Father Mario's background and I hired an investigator to... well, investigate. Once I learned the truth, it was not incumbent upon me to reveal it. My job was to ensure that Father Mario was innocent – which he was. I never believed it to be true from the onset and only conducted the investigation because the Church formality required it."

"What did your investigation reveal?"

Bishop Grogan shifted uncomfortably. He knew that, while Father Mario was bound by Church law not to reveal the truth, he was under no such authority. In fact, civil law now required him to confess what he did know. "The young boys were lovers."

Chief Johnson sat quietly for a moment, reflective. By this time, it was clear that the boys had been lovers. It was evidenced in the letter that Kevin had left for his parents; a letter that detailed a young life filled with pain, sadness and rejection. The letter had confirmed what Kevin's sister Caroline had confessed to him earlier in the day, rejection by his friends and family.

Kevin's letter had referenced his father's fury and disparaging taunts. He recounted how the hostility from his father would haunt him even in his dreams. In essence, Kevin's letter had been a documentary of growing up gay and his feelings of utter loneliness and despair at the loss of his best friend and first love, Michael.

Evidence of the boys' relationship had also been found in a video from Kevin's room. The video appeared to have had been made with the same camera that recorded Mrs. Conner's murder/suicide. In it, the boys were clearly enamored with each other. Using a tripod, the boys had recorded testimonials about how they came to know they were gay. They had described what it felt like to be ostracized, to have to act differently than how they felt inside. They had talked about the relief they felt to discover that they shared the same secret.

"How does proving the boys were in a relationship relieve Father Mario of guilt?" the Chief asked, even though he agreed with Bishop Grogan that the priest was innocent. He was digging to see if there was anything more.

"I guess it doesn't prove that he didn't do it. But there was no evidence to suggest he did."

Somehow, Chief Johnson's gut told him the Bishop was right. But for now, Father Mario was the only possible connection they had besides a phantom cleaning lady. For that reason, Chief Johnson had confidentially asked Father Mario to allow a DNA sample; an easy swab in the mouth if, for nothing else, to shut up Sarah Pulley.

Seemingly satisfied, the Chief stood up. "Shall we go visit Mrs. Larson?"

CHAPTER FORTY-NINE

There was a line of cars parked along the curb in front of the Larsons' home. Chief Johnson parked the patrol car behind the last one and Bishop Grogan pulled in behind him. As they made their way to the sidewalk of the house, the Chief filled the Bishop in on his earlier visit to give Mrs. Larson the news, and how it seemed she already knew. "Mothers always know," Bishop Grogan remarked, as they climbed the stairs to the house.

The woman who answered the door looked like a younger version of Jenny Larson. Chief Johnson introduced himself and Bishop Grogan. The woman, not surprisingly, turned out to be Jenny's younger sister Kelly. She invited them in and then went to tell Jenny they were here to see her. "We've had to give her something. She has just been hysterical all day," Kelly offered. She disappeared around the corner and several heads peeked out of the kitchen and nodded politely.

Kelly returned holding Jenny by the elbow. Chief Johnson was sure that when Jenny first saw him there was a light of hope in her eyes. *Another tragedy that people don't want to believe,* he thought. Kelly guided Jenny to the chair that twice she had occupied today in the Chief's presence. He offered the chair nearest Jenny to Bishop Grogan and he sat on the sofa.

Jenny's eyes were red and swollen. In the course of the day, her entire face had transformed from one of fear into one of anguish. In her lap she held tightly to a small, black leather-bound book, one he supposed held pictures of Kevin as a baby, pictures of his first steps, his first bicycle..."

Bishop Grogan reached gently for Jenny's hand and said a prayer for strength in adversity. As he prayed, the visitors who'd been sitting in the kitchen began filtering quietly into the living room, lining up against the wall. After the prayer, Bishop Grogan asked if Jenny had any questions for him. She shook her head slowly back and forth as if turning her head was painful.

Then, Bishop Grogan told Jenny about Father Patrick. He told her first about where the Irish priest had come from and how he had served the Church. He wanted Jenny to understand, if possible, the kind of man Father Patrick had been. He told her of the priest's compassion and how just this very morning, he'd consoled the Bishop himself. Then he told Jenny of Father Patrick's finding Kevin and his subsequent heart attack.

Gasps could be heard around the room and for a moment, the Chief thought his story telling was just adding more pain. Jenny's red-rimmed eyes welled with endless tears. Finally, Bishop Grogan told Jenny of Father Patrick's last words – that Kevin was standing at the river waiting to cross and that friends, grandparents and angels were waiting on the other side, beckoning him over. Bishop Grogan now understood that Father Patrick's last words had been spoken not to him, but to Kevin on the banks of the river. Bishop Grogan recounted the beautifully, mysterious story of how Father Patrick chose death over life so that he could go back to the river and show Kevin the way across.

"Mamma?" Jenny cried out, hearing the Bishop's reference to grandparents. "Daddy?" Jenny's body collapsed onto itself and Kelly, whose eyes were also wet with tears, raised her back up. "Thank you, thank you, thank you," Jenny sobbed, reaching out to Bishop Grogan. "My baby is safe, he's with mamma and daddy and the angels of glory. He's spared from the wrath of hell and damnation! He was a good child, a loving child and now he's in a better place, a kinder place!"

Chief Johnson was certain that if he didn't already have religion, he would have found it right then and there. As he looked around, there wasn't a dry eye in the room. Even he reached up and caught a little salt water that had found its way into his eyes. Bishop Grogan began another prayer. Afterwards, Jenny reached slowly for the book that had fallen from her lap moments earlier. As she settled in her chair she looked at the Bishop and offered him the book. "Forgive me, Bishop, for I have sinned. I have been a part of a something terrible."

"Would you like for us to find someplace private so you can confess?" the Bishop asked.

"No. I want to speak in front of all these witnesses. They are my friends and family and they love me." She held out the book to Bishop Grogan. "This is Kevin's diary. In it he speaks of his relationship with Michael Conner. He speaks of the two of them going to Father Mario to talk to him about their desires, their fears of going to hell, their fears of being outcast. There is nothing in here to implicate Father Mario of any wrong-doing.

He was just being a good priest and trying to counsel the boys. I found it yesterday after he stormed out of the house. I was going to tell the committee at the meeting yesterday that we had made a big mistake..." her voice trailed off.

Bishop Grogan took the book and thanked Jenny. "I guess you'll want this," he said, passing the book to Chief Johnson. Then turning back to Jenny, "This takes a lot of courage, Jenny. Thank you again."

She nodded and began to rise from her chair. Kelly quickly grabbed her by the elbow and held her steady. "Will you speak at his funeral, Bishop?"

Bishop Grogan stood and gently took Jenny's hand. "I will be coordinating Father Patrick's funeral, which will take place on Saturday. When do you wish to have Kevin's service?"

"Friday," she said, fresh tears streaming down her face.

"I will be honored."

Again, Jenny nodded her head and then turned to go back down the hall. When Kelly returned, she thanked the Bishop again and escorted the two men to the door. As they were leaving, Chief Johnson asked Kelly if Jenny's husband was home.

She looked startled and then replied cautiously, "No. Didn't Jenny tell you?"

"I guess not," the Chief responded. Although Kevin's sister Caroline had shared earlier that day that her father had threatened to beat the gayness out of his son, the Chief had learned over the years not to admit knowing anything. Information was never presented the same way by two people and new insight was almost always useful. He waited for Kelly to continue.

"Larry, her husband, had found porn on Kevin's computer. Pictures of men with men. He went crazy on Kevin, calling him every name in the book, telling he would disown him. He said a fag son wasn't worth having as a son."

She sighed and then added, "I think deep down Jenny knew about Kevin – that she'd suspected for a long time. But Jenny loved Kevin more than anything and his being gay wouldn't have stopped her love. She thinks that Larry is the reason why Kevin committed suicide."

"She knows, then?"

"Yes, the coroner confirmed it with a blood test. Plus, there was the note."

"So where is Larry?" he asked.

"We don't know. She kicked him out, accused him of killing Kevin. It's so sad, really... Everything is just so sad."

As Chief Johnson and Bishop Grogan walked back to their cars, the sun was sinking beyond the horizon. "Over the years, I've seen so many families broken up over a death," the Chief said.

Bishop Grogan nodded his head in understanding. "Yes, sometimes the tragedy seems to be too great."

"Especially when it comes down to a mother and her children," the Chief added. "I know the Good Book says that a husband and wife should love each other above anything else, but I just don't think that's natural. I think nothing is greater than love between a mother and a child."

"Do you have children?" Bishop Grogan asked.

"No. I'm too selfish. I couldn't imagine my wife loving anyone more than me," he replied, smiling at the Bishop.

Bishop Grogan nodded and smiled back. He reached out and

shook the Chief's hand. "Goodnight, Chief Johnson."

"Goodnight, Bishop Grogan."

CHAPTER FIFTY

When Chief Johnson arrived at the station the next morning at 0600, he walked into more than a dozen leads to the Conner murders from all over the country. Although Julia had left him a voice message telling him that the story went out over wire at 1800 the evening before, he had not seen it until he read the morning paper.

Little did he know that Julia Frank's story about Calvin, the black cocker spaniel who had lost his family to a brutal murder and then disappeared without a trace, was one of the most emailed, Facebooked and Tweeted stories floating around cyberspace.

Chief Johnson sat down to sort through the leads with a smile on his face. *Gotta go with the gut,* he thought. *It never does you wrong.* He reached over to an aging stereo that sat on a table in his office among piles of papers, files and boxes of things he had long forgotten. Like his car, Darlene, he found himself attached to the beauty of the past. He pressed a silver button that started the cassette tape inside to spin. A moment later the deep, bluesy voice of Albert King filled the room.

He would look first for local leads or anything coming out of the Southwest where the voice analysts suggested the person reporting the crime had originated. He couldn't help but think back to Zach's singing the little Southwest jingle, *"Arizona, New Mexico, Oklahoma, Texas."* He knew that Zach might be young and green around the gills, but he was bright – not to mention resourceful.

Just as he began reading one of local leads, the dispatcher was at his door.

"Chief, there's a call on line one. Guy in Newport News says his neighbor recently sold a car to a woman who had a black cocker spaniel with her."

"Life is good, Corporal. We're going to solve this case before the week is out." He smiled and picked up the phone.

Twenty minutes later, the Chief was in the briefing room, updating the war board for the 0700 meeting. The phone call had proved very interesting and as soon as the morning brief was over, he'd be heading out to investigate further. Yes, he could send Lacey or any other of the officers, but he just couldn't let go of the thrill of the hunt. He was a police chief who had to be in on the action. The other leads had not looked so promising, but he'd thought one might yield information worthy of consideration. He would give that one to someone else to follow up on. *Gotta share the adventure*, he thought cheerfully.

While he waited for the men and women of the Hampton Police Department to filter in, he grabbed a string cheese from the grocery bag in the center table up front. He knew better than to wait until after the briefing. He reached down to pull his phone from its clip on his belt. It was a text from the lovely Julia.

Thanks 4 the lead. Story picked up across US – 1 of 25 most-read stories posted in last 24 hrs. Expect it to be top 10 b4 EOD

The Chief smiled and typed out his response.

TYS

A question mark was texted back a moment later.

He had to spell it out for her. Yes, he needed to reinforce his experience and intuitive skill to the novice young-blood. He laughed heartedly as he pressed send.

Told you so! Statement at 1100. Promise

As his team was assembling, Lieutenant Eaton rummaged through the goodie bag.

"Thanks Chief!" he said, pulling out the strawberry-banana yogurt.

"No prob, Eaton, anything I can do to help you lose that belly," he replied with a chuckle. "There's strawberry-kiwi too."

He checked his watch and compared it to the clock that hung on the wall in the back of the room. *Close enough,* he thought. "Okay, team, let's get started. Lots to do to catch up with the wildfire that Julia Frank's "Calvin" story started. "How many of you read this morning's paper?"

Several hands went up.

"What'd ya think?" he asked. "Anybody shed a tear or two?" he asked teasingly.

"Good story," Sergeant Walker offered. "I was surprised at how in touch with dog psychology she seemed to be."

"That's the magic of a good story-writer," the Chief responded. "Who else? C'mon, don't tell me I've got a team of illiterates. Please tell me you read the daily, at least! Lacey, did you read it?"

George Lacey lifted the paper from the table and waved it around as if that answered the Chief's question. When his gaze didn't move away, Lacey coughed nervously. "I don't typically follow Ms. Frank's writing, but yes, I read the story and yes, I thought it was well done. I guess it will move the animal lovers. Not much for the intellectual, but I guess we're driving for an emotional response with this story, right?"

Chief Johnson smiled and nodded his agreement. He knew that Lacey didn't like Julia and he knew that love affair went both ways. Observation of human behavior fascinated him and he'd often thought that if he'd been able to afford to go to college when he'd gotten out of high school instead of taking classes here and there during his early years on the police force, he'd have been a psychologist. In reality, the force offered him a taste of just about everything. *Life is as is should be,* he often reminded himself. "Okay, before 0900, I want every one of you to have read the story. You all embarrass me sometimes."

"I was going to get to it, Chief. I'm just not much of a morning person. Gotta have a couple of cups of java and then I'm all into it," Zach offered, a big smile plastered on his freshly shaven face.

"Good to know, Zach. I'll tell the city of Hampton to stay on their best behavior until 0900 just for you," he chided. "Now, let's get down to business. We all sat here at the end of the day yesterday, but a lot has happened since then. Most important is

225

that our story is out in print and on wire. I came in to a dozen or so leads, two of which look promising. I'm going to be heading out this morning to talk to one up near Newport News and there's one from down near Fayetteville, North Carolina, that I want someone to follow up on.

"I'll take it," the Chief heard several voices offer simultaneously. He looked around the room to identify the folks wanting a piece of the action and offered it to Lieutenant Jennifer Sanders, a new member to the team who was smart as a whip and not one to mess with. The Chief had seen her lay out half a dozen of his men, one right after the other, at the last self-defense workshop.

"Sanders, it's yours," the Chief said. "Next. We need follow up with Sarah Pulley. Gotta get those names and see if we can find out who that cleaning lady is. Lacey, that's you after *your bad* from yesterday."

"Got it, Chief."

"Eaton, keep working forensics will you. Every time they come up with anything interesting I want to know."

"Yes, sir."

"As you know, a young man by the name of Kevin Larson was reported missing yesterday morning and later found dead at St. Joseph's. Looks like suicide. Any update on that?"

"Blood test revealed OD on pain killers and alcohol," said Eaton. "Not to mention, his letter was a note to his family apologizing for being an embarrassment and telling them he couldn't live as someone else for the rest of his life. Pretty sad really. Especially being so young."

The Chief didn't hear anything that surprised him, he'd expected as much. Besides, he'd already read the letter. "Kevin

Larson and Michael Conner, the oldest of the three Conner boys, were having an intimate relationship," the Chief clarified. "I learned yesterday from Kevin's sister that the father recently outed Kevin and humiliated him – pretty much disowned him. Both Mr. and Mrs. Larson were part of the committee, as were Mr. and Mrs. Conner, that was trying to oust Father Mario, the priest at St. Joseph's. Last evening Mrs. Larson turned over Kevin's diary and stated that the priest was not guilty of any illicit behavior; but was instead, just counseling the two young lovers through their issues."

Chief Johnson picked up the small, black book from the table that he leaned against and held it up. "There was a reference, however, to a woman who continued to proselytize and condemn their affection for each other. I read through it last night and would like for another pair of eyes to have a read."

Several hands shot up. "Okay, you bunch of perverts... I just need one volunteer for the time being." He walked over and handed the book to Zach, whose face deepened to crimson.

"But Chief, I didn't raise my hand..."

"I know you didn't raise your hand, that's why I'm giving it to you. I want you to read it while I'm working this one lead and then I want you to give me your thoughts about possible connections when I get back. I've been really impressed with you lately. I want to know if you can consistently report good police insight or if you just got lucky before."

"Yes, sir."

"Anything more on the disks that came out of Kevin's room?" the Chief asked, turning his attention to Sergeant Walker.

"Yes, I believe we've found something that may be of interest.

I've turned it over to the tech guru for confirmation, but I believe that the recording of Mrs. Conner's death was recorded over the same video the boys made of themselves. The same video we found in Kevin's room."

"Now we're getting somewhere," the Chief said, as he added more notes to the white board. "Tell folks about the boys' documentary. We need everyone's thinking on this one."

"Michael Conner and Kevin Larsen were interviewing each other. They asked questions about likes, dislikes, love, family and how it felt to be different," Sergeant Walker began. He paused a moment while he thought back to his viewing of the tape. He had watched it repeatedly for both professional and personal reasons. Professionally, he knew he'd found something of importance. Personally, he had felt moved by the words.

"And..." Chief Johnson said, bringing Sergeant Walker back into the present.

"Well, at the beginning of the video we found at the Conner home, there are a couple of seconds where the camera is being moved and just a millisecond of sound. At the beginning of the DVD we found in Kevin's room there is a similar shuffling at the beginning of the disk, followed by laughter as the boys set up to begin their interviews."

"So, what's the significance?" came the questions from several officers.

"The significance is *why* or *how* did the murderer choose this particular video to record this horrible end to what was once a happy, loving family?" came George Lacey's response.

"Exactly," confirmed Sergeant Walker. Especially if you consider that the murder video doesn't start at the beginning of the tape, but about a third of the way through."

The room was quiet as minds worked to incorporate this information into the profile they were building of a killer. "If the killer did deliberately record over the video of the boys, what significance could that have?" asked Lieutenant Sanders.

"Could have been a coincidence," offered Michaels.

"Possible, of course, but I think unlikely," the Chief rebutted. "Next."

"Maybe the cleaning lady is the same one who was proselytizing to them. Maybe this is a hate crime, of sorts," offered Sergeant Walker.

At the mention of hate crime, the thought of the threats against Father Mario came to mind. "That's certainly a possibility," offered the Chief. "Let's see if we can find a connection."

"The murderer wanted to erase the boys' interview. Was there anything in Kevin's disk to implicate anyone?" Zach asked.

Sergeant Walker reflected and then told the room about the boys' rejection from peers at school. "They didn't reference anyone in particular, with the exception of their fathers. Both boys feared rejection by their families who condemned homosexuality. But, Kevin seemed especially fearful of his father."

"Speaking of Kevin's father," the Chief interjected, "I want someone tracking Larry Larson. I learned last night that Mrs. Larson kicked him out of the house and is blaming him for Kevin's suicide. He works at GTech Networks at Buckroe Beach. I want two officers tracking him day and night. See if you can talk to anyone who might know him. Let's see who we're dealing with here and if there's reason to consider him a suspect in the Conner murders. You never know with these kinds of things."

The Chief nodded at the volunteers from the back of the room. "Keep me posted on anything and everything."

He looked around the room, not so much to check their understanding but to prompt his memory for anything he might have neglected to mention. "Anything else?"

"So, is the priest off the hook?"

"Nobody's off the hook until we've nailed the killer."

"What's the lead you have in Newport News? Wasn't that the area where the call was received reporting the murders?"

"A man says his neighbor sold a car to a woman who had a black cocker spaniel. He says he saw her because it was on the fourth of July and he was out back grilling." I'm going out to have a look around the neighborhood, talk to the neighbor, see if anyone else saw her. Check out who we're dealing with."

"What's the connection to the Fayetteville lead?"

"Guy says he helped a woman with a flat tire. Older woman, silver hair. She had a black cocker spaniel in the back of her car."

"It'd be too easy for those two to be connected. But wouldn't it be sweet," Lieutenant Sanders said.

Chief Johnson thought for a moment as if measuring how he would respond. "Sometimes life is sweet," he offered. "Bitter sweet."

CHAPTER FIFTY-ONE

Father Mario slept better than he had in days. He woke up and looked around the guest room he continued to occupy. When Bishop Grogan had joined them, it was already late in the evening but the two priests had waited for his return before having dinner. The Bishop didn't waste any time telling Father Mario about his visit with Mrs. Larson and her revelation about Kevin's diary.

Father Mario couldn't describe the relief he felt – as if the weight of the world had been lifted from his shoulders. But with that relief came a deep sadness. In his mind, he saw both Michael and Kevin sitting in front of him, sharing their situation and the depth of their feelings for each other. He knew they were both young, but he accepted this as their "first love."

Even though the church did not condone homosexuality, it was still his responsibility as their priest to counsel and console them. How could he have betrayed that trust to explain his involvement in the situation? Given the controversy about the Catholic priests and young boys, who would have believed him anyway?

Although the Bishop told Father Mario that he could return to his duties at St. Joseph's effective immediately, he wasn't sure how he would feel going back to face a congregation who, for the most part, had believed the worst of him. When Father Mario asked Bishop Grogan's counsel for how to best move himself and the congregation past this bitter memory, he had suggested prayer. If anything would test Father Mario's resolve, not to mention his commitment to the church, moving beyond this tragedy would be it.

Father Mario sat up in the bed and found himself staring again at the painted feathers. He stood, stretched and reached for his slacks at the foot of the bed. As he dressed, he eyed the paintings, wondering what it was about painted feathers that interested him so much. Finally giving in to curiosity, he once again stood in front of the two frames and explored the details of each feather. He shook his head at the beauty. *So hard to believe that all of this is painted on the feather of a bird*, he thought. Then looking down in the corner of one of the frames he noticed the artist's name. *Where have I heard that name before?* Then he remembered.

Father Mario quickly opened the door to his room and wasn't surprised to see the Bishop's door open and his room looking as though it had never been occupied. The Bishop had mentioned the evening before that he wanted to get an early start since there was much to do in coordinating the move of Father Patrick's body back to Richmond. Plus, he had promised to be at Kevin's funeral on Friday. Father Mario went quickly down the stairs and into the kitchen where Margaret was preparing breakfast. "Is Father Cameron up yet?"

"Yes, he's taking his coffee on the back porch this morning. Shall I pour you a cup?"

"Thanks, I'll get it," Father Mario replied, reaching for a cup already resting next to the coffee pot.

He joined Father Cameron on the back deck and as soon as the morning greetings were complete, he began his questioning. He asked first for the name of the woman who had donated the home to the Church – Louisa Armstrong. Then he asked Father Cameron the name of the woman he had once loved – Liz Grant. A smile spread across Father Mario's face, inspiring Father Cameron to ask what was up.

"Two more questions and then I'll tell you. First question: You never knew Louisa Armstrong, right?

"Right."

"Second question: Neither you nor anyone else ever knew why Louisa Armstrong left the house to the Church – if I recall, she wasn't even Catholic.

"Right again," Father Cameron responded. "So there are your two questions, what's going on?"

"Louisa Elizabeth Grant Armstrong, that's what."

Father Cameron looked at Father Mario, confusion written all over his face. "I don't get it."

"Come with me," Father Mario said with excitement, jumping up from the step and looking back to ensure his friend was following. They both placed their coffee cups on the kitchen counter as they passed through and made their way up the stairs and into the guest room. "Have you ever looked at these?" Father Mario asked, pointing to the frames holding the painted feathers.

"I've seen them but I guess I've never really looked at them that closely. They weren't part of the auction because they were to stay with the house. There were several things that were part of the house and not to be auctioned – furniture, odds and ends. So, what does this have to do with anything?"

"Look at the artist's signature."

Father Cameron moved closer the frames, adjusted his glasses and leaned forward. Father Mario watched him straighten up and then lean forward again as if not trusting his own eyes. "It can't be," Father Cameron said softly, lifting one of the frames from the wall to examine it more closely. "I must ask Margaret."

The two men moved back down the stairs and into the kitchen, Father Cameron carrying one of the frames. "Margaret, what can you tell us about these painted feathers?" he asked.

Margaret turned and, after seeing what he held, smiled sadly. "Mrs. Louisa was a brilliant artist, was she not?"

"Yes, it's brilliant. I had no idea this was her work," Father Cameron replied. "I see that she signed her name Louisa Elizabeth Grant Armstrong. Did she ever go by Elizabeth Grant?"

"Grant was her maiden name. Before she married Mr. Armstrong she went by Liz Grant."

Father Cameron's mind couldn't put it together fast enough. He stood as if in a state of frozen confusion. Finally Margaret broke the silence, "Father, are you just putting all this together?"

Father Cameron's head jerked up and he studied Margaret closely. "You mean you knew all along?"

"Of course I knew. Mrs. Louisa told me after Mr. Armstrong died."

"But you never said anything!"

"I didn't think it was my place, Father."

"Yes, I suppose you are right. I just never put the two together, that's all." He turned slowly and went into his study where he placed the framed feathers on his desk. He walked over to the windows and looked out over the garden in the back yard. All the times he had stood here and wondered about the woman who had lived in this house before him. He knew her all along – he had loved her all along.

CHAPTER FIFTY-TWO

Chief Johnson and Sergeant Walker pulled up to the Newport News home where, supposedly, the occupant had recently sold an auto to a woman with a black cocker spaniel. The Chief had insisted on driving, as he always did. "I know the roads better," was his standard phrase. The two men got out of the patrol car and walked up the drive to the front porch and rang the bell. A moment later, a Hispanic woman opened the door, eyes frightened to find two police officers at her door.

"Sí?"

"Habla English?"

"No. No English."

Chief looked at Sergeant Walker. "How good is your Spanish?"

"I can hold my own okay."

"Ask if her husband is home."

"¿Estas su marido a casa?"

"No, él trabaja."

"She says he's working," Sergeant Walker translated.

"Ask if they recently sold a car to a woman with a black dog."

"¿Vendió recientemente usted un coche a una mujer con un perro negro?"

"Sí," she answered with a shy smile. "El perro era mono."

"She said yes and that the dog was cute or something... I'm not sure I understood."

"Ask her what kind of car."

"¿Qué tipo de coche le hizo venta?"

"Un Mercury Sable. Verde."

"Green Mercury Sable," the Chief repeated. "The same make, model and color of the report near Fayetteville. Ask her when they sold the car and what the woman looked like. Ask if there were any unusual characteristics about her. Anything out of the ordinary."

"¿Cuándo le hizo venta el coche?"

"Ella pagó la mitad el dinero el cuarto de julio y luego volvió hace dos días con el resto. Era muy tarde por la noche. Dormíamos cuando ella llamó en la puerta."

"Haga usted recuerda algo extraño sobre la mujer. ¿Algo que podría ayudarnos a encontrarla?"

"No de lamentable," she said, shaking her head.

"¿A qué pareció ella? ¿Qué edad?"

"Pelo de plata corto. Más viejo pero no sé que edad."

"She says the woman paid half the money on July fourth and then came two days ago late in the night with the rest of the money. She doesn't recall anything but says the woman had short silver hair and was older. She's not sure about age." Sergeant Walker translated.

Then he turned back to the woman and asked in Spanish how the dog acted when he was here and if the dog was present two nights ago as well. He turned to the Chief and translated her response. The dog had looked frightened on both occasions.

"I think we have our prime suspect," the Chief remarked. "Now, if we just knew who she was, where she came from and where she's headed." Turning to the woman, he offered his thanks. She nodded and smiled, quickly closed the door and clicked the lock.

Sergeant Walker was already making notes as Chief Johnson started the car and turned it around to head back to Hampton. The two were debating the profile of a silver-haired woman murderess and dog-napper when the Chief's phone rang. He answered and then pulled the car slowly off to the side of the road.

"What the hell does that mean?" Chief asked into the phone. He waited for an explanation. "I'll be damned. Anything else?" When he ended the call, he was shaking his head. "You just never know, you just never know..."

Sergeant Walker waited patiently for him to elaborate. After the car was back on the road, the Chief looked over at Sergeant Walker to offer some explanation. "I had Father Mario do a swab test – you know, just to cover the bases. You're not going to believe this. You remember the tissue on the trash? Well, the priest's DNA is not a one hundred percent match, but there is a lot of code that is identical. Forensics says that, if the tissue is from the killer, then the killer has a high probability of being directly related to Father Mario."

Sergeant Walker nodded his head with the news. "I guess we need to go back and ask him a few more questions."

"Yes. Yes, we do. Oh, and the Fayetteville lead said the

woman he helped was driving a green Mercury Sable. Her tire had blown, but he found a worn spare in the back. He said the dog was crying something terrible the whole time and when he looked in the back to get the spare that the dog had shit its cage."

CHAPTER FIFTY-THREE

Father Mario sat silently in the passenger seat as Father Cameron drove him back to St. Joseph's where his car had been parked since the day before. The few moments of pleasure he had enjoyed solving the Louisa Armstrong benefactor mystery had been quickly replaced with the reality of his own life. His return to a congregation of doubters, to a congregation that thought the worst of him. As if this wasn't enough, he also had the loss of the Conner family, plus Kevin. *How can I help the church family heal when I don't know if I can heal myself?* he wondered.

Father Cameron turned into the parking lot of St. Joseph's and parked next to Father Mario's car. Both men's eyes were on the police car parked near the entrance. Only one other car was in the lot and Father Mario immediately recognized it as Sarah Pulley's. Just yesterday they had pulled into the parking lot and met with tragedy. Today, Father Mario felt a renewed fear that made his heart beat faster.

"How about I go in with you – just to make sure you get settled," Father Cameron offered.

Father Mario sighed deeply. "No, you've done enough. I can manage; but thanks just the same. I really appreciate everything." Father Mario looked over at his friend and gave him a sad smile before opening the door and climbing out of the car. For a moment he hesitated on the sidewalk, trying to decide if he should go into his house or the church first. Finally, feeling Father Cameron's eyes on him, he headed toward the big, wooden door that led into the church – his church.

Inside, the air was cool and smelled faintly of incense. He walked toward the office where he heard voices – one he recognized as Sarah's. As he approached, the voices stopped and the man, an officer whom he first met at the Conners' home two days earlier when he'd made that fateful trip to confirm his worst fears, stood up to greet him.

"Father Mario, in case you don't remember me, I'm investigator George Lacey with the Hampton Police Department." He extended his hand.

"Yes. I remember," Father Mario replied, reaching his hand in greeting. "Is everything okay?"

"Yes. I was just following up with Ms. Pulley to get information about some of the parishioners. If you have just a minute, I'd like to ask you a couple more questions."

"Sure," Father Mario said, nodding his head. He looked at Sarah who was glaring at him. "Thank you for doing so much to help out the last few days Sarah." He hesitated, then asked, "Are you okay?"

Sarah looked down at the desk and didn't respond.

"Sarah?" Father Mario asked again and then it dawned on him. Sarah Pulley was one of them – one of the members who had been trying to oust him. He couldn't hide the sour look that passed across his face. "I'll be in my office whenever you're ready," he said, turning back to officer Lacey.

"Actually, I've finished up here. Can I join you now?" officer Lacey asked, standing up to follow.

"Of course," Father Mario replied. Then, turning back to Sarah he added, "Why don't you take the rest of the day off, Sarah? You've had quite a lot of stress piled on you lately. We can pick back up tomorrow morning."

Without a word, Sarah reached for her handbag and headed toward the door.

The two men settled into Father Mario's office and the priest looked across his desk anxiously. "Chief Johnson told us about Kevin Larson's diary and that his mother spoke up in your defense. I'm really glad to hear that," officer Lacey began.

"I hate that my vindication came at Kevin's expense," Father Mario said, his voice carrying the sadness in his heart.

"Yes, this has been a sad set of events all the way around." officer Lacey offered. "Just a couple more questions and I'll be out of your way. For starters, do you recall any new members in your church in the past few months?"

Father Mario thought for a minute but shook his head. "We have new faces every Sunday. When new members join, we have a welcome committee that invites them to a reception that I always attend. Most new members attend the session, but not all. I believe it's been a couple of months since our last one."

"Given the situation with the Conner and Larson boys, can you think of anyone who would want to hurt them or their family?"

Father Mario shook his head. There was no way he could

fathom someone with such brutal intentions. "No, this kind of thinking is beyond my understanding."

Just as officer Lacey was getting ready to stand, his cell phone rang. "Lacey," he said into the phone before hanging in silence for what seemed to Father Mario like an eternity. Officer Lacey was looking at Father Mario when he closed his cell phone and offered an apology for the interruption. "Can't just ignore the phone when you're with the force," he said, apologetically.

Father Mario nodded his head but said nothing, waiting for whatever was next.

"I know that both Sergeant Walker and Chief Johnson talked to you yesterday so again, I just want to thank you for your time again today," officer Lacey said, trying to warm up to the question he really needed to ask next. "Just out of curiosity, being a priest and all, do you have any family nearby – I mean, like brothers, sisters, parents?"

"I'm an only son and my mother is in Texas. I haven't seen my father since I was a young boy."

"Must get lonely sometimes. I don't know about you, but if I don't talk to my mother at least once a week I feel like a terrible son! How about you?"

Father Mario looked visibly uncomfortable as he shifted position in his chair. "I guess my mother and I are comfortable with less frequent chats," he said.

"Oh. Well, that's how it is sometimes I guess. So, where 'bouts in Texas? I've got family out near Austin myself."

"Quanah. Small town nobody's ever heard of," Father Mario offered.

"Last time I was in Texas was a couple of years ago. Can't

believe how fast things change. I bet even Quanah's changed."

"Maybe."

"Well, I've taken up enough of your time today," officer Lacey said, standing. "If you think of anything that might be helpful, you'll let us know?"

"Yes, of course. I'll do whatever I can," Father Mario said, standing to walk the police officer to the door.

"Oh, one thing I forgot," he said, turning back to Father Mario. "I know we've asked you this question a few times already, but just to make sure... When was the last time you were at the Conner home? Not counting two days ago."

Father Mario thought for a moment before responding. "I think I was there about a year ago for a church meeting the Conners were hosting."

"That's what's so strange," said officer Lacey. "Forensics found a DNA sample from the Conners' home that almost matches yours. If it didn't belong to you, it must belong to an immediate family member. Who do you think that would be?"

Father Mario visibly stumbled before finding his chair and sitting down. "Come again? I'm not sure I'm following what you just said."

"Let me make it easier for you. If you have any family, we need to know who they are and where they live. And when we find them, we'll need to take a DNA sample."

"All I have is my mother, just like I said, and she lives in Quanah, Texas. 104 Main Street. I have no idea where my father is or even if he's still living."

"Any chance I could get a photo from you of your mother?"

The disbelief Father Mario felt two days ago when he realized he was a murder suspect returned so suddenly he felt as though he'd been punched in the stomach. This time he realized that police were looking at his mother as a suspect. "I only have a couple of photos – from about seven years ago. They're in the parsonage next door."

"Can we walk over now? I'll like to borrow one or two; I'll make sure to return them to you tomorrow."

Numbly, Father Mario opened the wooden door to the church and led the way down the sidewalk and around the side to where his little home, most recently occupied by Father Patrick, stood waiting for him. He fumbled for his door key and realized, as he inserted the key into the lock, that his hands were shaking. Once inside, Father Mario walked to a small bookcase in the front room of the house and pulled from the lower shelf a small photo album. He turned a few pages before pausing. Then slowly, he pulled the clear plastic from its sticky backing and lifted a photo out of the book. He passed it over to officer Lacey who looked at it with interest. Looking at Father Mario he nodded. "I can see the resemblance," he said.

Father Mario slowly closed the book and placed it back on the lower shelf. "Anything else?" he asked.

Investigator George Lacey considered the priest for a moment. Then, shaking his head and turning toward the door he answered. "No, I think that's it for now. Thanks again and sorry about all this. Just a formality, you know."

"Sure," Father Mario said, disbelief setting in.

CHAPTER FIFTY-FOUR

When Chief Johnson and Sergeant Walker returned to the station, Zach was holding the phone between his ear and shoulder, waving his arms like a madman. The Chief walked over just as Zach placed the phone back in its cradle.

"Calvin, the infamous cocker spaniel, has been found in Dillon, SC. That was the Veterinary Hospital. They said a family found him in his cage off the side of Interstate 95, about twenty miles from their clinic. Positive identification based on the tag the dog was wearing. Had his name and home address."

The Chief's smile was as wide as his face. "Now, we're getting somewhere! Gotta love it when the dog-napper neglects to remove the positive identification."

"That was the good news," Zach continued. "Bad news is the dog's in pretty bad shape and they don't know if he'll make it. Dehydration, shock and a few other words that only a doctor can say."

"We'll want to contact the Dillon police department and get someone over there to run prints on the crate. There's probably twenty different prints on it by now, but let's do it ASAP. We also need to talk to the family that found him and get an exact location of where the dog was found. Let's see what else we might be able to find out there, tire tracks... Anything. So, it looks like what we've got is a woman who took the dog, heading south. I wonder why she dumped the dog."

"I wonder why she took the dog in the first place." Zach asked. "As for why she dumped it, the vet says he was covered in shit. Already had flies laying maggots – he'd been outside for a day, they're guessing. They think he must have gotten diarrhea while he was in the car and the dog-napper didn't know what to do and couldn't stand the stench."

"Who brought him in? Possible connection?"

"Doesn't sound like it, Chief. A family from Chapel Hill was headed to the beach and the eight-year old son had to stop for a piss. He spotted the cage as he watered the side of the road. The vet said the little boy is traumatized over the condition of the dog and begged his mom to let him stay to make sure the dog makes it. The vet said the dad pitched a big one. Was all pissed about the stinking dog in the back of the SUV, pissed that they were going to lose half a day at the beach. Apparently, he and the mom had quite a row over the whole thing. The dad finally took the other son and went to the beach without them. Mom and the youngest son are staying at a nearby bed and breakfast."

"Can't make that kind of story up."

"Yeah, that's what I was thinking."

Chief Johnson looked at his watch; forty-five minutes until he promised Ms. Frank a statement. "Okay, let's have a quick assembly before the press gets here. Someone give Lacey a call and see how soon he'll get back. Hopefully he'll have a photo for us. Also, get me someone from forensics. I need an expert to explain that mitochondrial-DNA thing. I'd sound like an idiot trying to talk science."

"Chief, I've got Texas law enforcement on the line for you."

The Chief ran the short distance to his office; this case was heating up and the speed at which things were coming together didn't leave a moment to spare. The DNA hit had been big, and although he couldn't explain the science, he understood that mitochondria passed from mother to son – a genetic marker that didn't change. The tissue from the scene had contained not only nasal fluid and discarded cells, but also blood.

Although the DNA profile between the tissue sample and Father Mario wasn't a perfect match, there were a couple of locus repeats. Most important, the mitochondrial DNA had been a perfect match. That meant only one thing. This tissue sample had to have come from Father Stephen Mario's mother who, he had said in his interview just yesterday, was supposed to be in Quanah, Texas.

When the Chief finished his call and came back out of his office, officer Lacey had returned. He called his staff into the war room and gave them the latest news. "Ladies and gentlemen, I just got off the phone with Hardeman County Sheriff Danny Pickens. When I learned earlier about the DNA hit, I thought it would be a good idea to see if there was anything of interest from Texas. Turns out, I was right."

"Again," he heard several voices call out.

Chief Johnson laughed. "Yes, and that's why I'm Chief and you're not." He waited for the laughter to settle before he

248

continued. "Seriously though, we've hit a hot one here. Seems that Father Mario's mother, Constance Franklin Mario, left Quanah about eight months ago after the sheriff's department questioned her regarding a possible connection to a poisoning death of Darius Cash. Apparently, she had some history with Mr. Cash who, after finding Jesus, needed to come clean on a crime that he had committed many years ago at her request."

"Jesus is the answer!" came a cheer from the back.

"Okay, pay attention. According to Mr. Cash's daughter, Constance Mario hired him to off her husband Roland about 25 years ago."

"How did the daughter know?" came the question from several officers.

"The daughter had been staying with him, thinking he was sick with the flu. His condition worsened and before he died, he confessed. According to the story, Mr. Cash told Constance Mario that he was going to come clean since he had become a Christian. He thought maybe he could convince her to repent her sins, too. The daughter didn't think her father was in his right mind when he gave his deathbed confession, but she went to Sheriff Pickens, who had been a friend of the family. The Sheriff immediately ordered an autopsy of Mr. Cash – the results of which were toxic levels of ethylene glycol."

"Hard to believe folks are still using antifreeze," Zach remarked. "Especially when it's so easy to pinpoint in an autopsy."

"The Sheriff was cautious with the case because he didn't know which woman was guilty. The daughter, who came to him with the story, was the sole benefactor of her father's insurance policy – wasn't much, but still. This same daughter is a single mother who had recently lost her job and was about to have her car repossessed. It didn't look very pretty. When the Sheriff realized that Constance Mario had cleaned out and left town, he started to consider the daughter's story as possibly legit."

"So what's the next step?" officer Lacey asked.

"How long will it take to scan Constance Mario's photo and put a short silver wig-do on her?" the Chief asked, looking at Corporal Nate Day, the resident computer graphics guru.

"Do you have a description of what the wig-do looks like?" Corporal Day asked.

"Got a description from Sarah Pulley of a woman who was relatively new to the parish, short silver hair – said her name was Ruth Christian. She didn't give an address on file, had said she was still looking for a permanent place to call home. By the way, the woman who fits the description was on the committee trying to oust the priest. That'd be kind of strange if she was trying to oust her own son," said Lacey.

The Chief considered this new information and began his mental exercise of piecing it into the puzzle that already lay, partly assembled, in his mind. "You never know about these things," he said. "I've seen stranger things happen. So, how did Sarah Pulley describe her?"

Pulling out his notes, officer Lacey ran his finger down the page and then recited, "Chin length bob, bangs and short tapering in the back. Sixty-ish."

"Color?" asked Corporal Day, making notes.

"Silver-ish," officer Lacey responded.

"Silver-ish?" Corporal Day asked.

"Silver-ish," Lacey repeated.

"Lots of –ishes in this description," the Corporal commented under his breath. "Fifteen minutes," he said, looking at the Chief.

"Excellent timing, Corporal Day, because that's exactly how much time you have."

CHAPTER FIFTY-FIVE

Father Mario sat on the sofa in the small living room of the parsonage and looked through his photo album. For every picture he found of his mother, he focused hard as if the image would reveal to him some mystery. *Do I really know who she is?* He asked himself. *Really?*

His memories of his mother could be described as follows: very religious, overly-protective and introverted. She preached to Father Mario on every occasion from the time he can remember. "You got to love God first and foremost," he remembered her saying. "Love and serve the Lord God with all your heart and all your soul." *Could a woman who was intent on serving God with all her heart and soul be capable of something so heinous?* he wondered in disbelief.

As a teenager, she never let him spend the night with friends, thinking that he would make immoral judgments. "Temptation comes from our own desires, which entice us and drag us away," she would quote from James, and when he asked why she always quoted that verse to him she would simply reply, "Be on your guard. Your enemy the devil is like a roaring lion. He prowls around looking for someone to chew up and swallow."

His memories of his mother were of church – working for the church, going to church and quoting the Bible. How could this Godly woman be guilty of murder? There must be some mistake!

Father Mario went to his desk and dialed the number that had belonged to the little house on Main Street for as long as he could remember.

"The number you have dialed has been disconnected," came the automated response.

"What?" he heard himself exclaim out loud. He dialed the number again and listened to a repeat of the message. Opening the top drawer of the desk he pulled out a small, blue notebook with alphabetized pages. Flipping through until he got to L, he ran his finger down the few entries and stopped on Flora Lovette, his mother's sister, who lived in Aynor, South Carolina. He hadn't spoken to her in years, since before he went to seminary. Desperate, he dialed her number and held his breath. On the third ring, she answered.

"Aunt Flora, this is Stephen. Stephen Mario. I know it's been a long time."

"Stephen, well bless my soul! I can't believe it's actually you. Your mother and I were just talking about you!"

"You were just talking to my mother? Were you on the phone?" he asked, hoping that instead of her line being disconnected, it had just been busy and the telephone company had crossed the recordings.

"Why Lord no, son, she's here visiting. Would you like to speak to her?"

"Yes, thank you Aunt Flora." His mind was spinning. What did this mean? What would he say to her?

When he heard his mother's voice over the line, his heart jumped. It was the same voice he always remembered – soft and carrying a distant echo of sadness. He felt suddenly protective of her.

"Mom, I just tried calling you at home and I got a recording that said the phone had been disconnected. Is everything all right?"

"Yes, everything is fine. I didn't think it made sense to keep it connected while I'm off visiting family."

"How long have you been with Flora?"

"Not too long at all, it's good to catch up. So how are you, dear?"

"How did you get out there? Did you take the bus?"

"Yes, it was a long ride but nice. I enjoy seeing the country side," she said, her voice carrying a hint of excitement for her adventure.

He couldn't remember her ever taking a long trip before, especially so far from home. "Mom, did you by chance pass through the Hampton area?"

"Now wouldn't I have stopped in to see you if I'd been there?" she asked sincerely.

More confused than ever, Father Mario didn't have a response.

"Is everything okay, dear? Your voice sounds different."

He wondered how his mother could make such a statement given that they hardly conversed at all. They might speak on the phone once or twice a year. *How could she know if my voice sounded different?* he wondered. One minute he's feeling protective of his mother and the next minute he feels irritation. "I've had a rough week," he said at last. "Not one I ever hope to repeat." Then, trying to figure out what to say next he changed the subject. "How long will you be there with Flora? Do you have a return bus ticket yet?"

"For the first time in my life, I don't have a plan. I'll stay here in Aynor for a bit and visit with Flora. Then, I'll mosey on. Where to, I'm not sure."

"Why don't I drive down to visit both of you," he suggested, feeling desperate. "I could drive down in less than six hours." Somehow he felt that seeing his mother, sitting in the same room with her, would give him a better sense for what was going on. Why would she have made such a long trip east without even telling him? Why didn't she have any plans to return? His mother always had a plan. When to get up, what to do, where to go, how long it should take, what was needed for dinner. He held his breath waiting for her answer.

"You know how I hate seeing you in that death garb," she said, referring to his black slacks and shirt and white collar. Her tone had turned sour. "It breaks my heart knowing that you are throwing away your soul to the devil. Can't you see the evil in that Church of yours? It's in the news every day – the Catholic Church is an embarrassment to Christianity. Aren't you humiliated to be a part of something so evil?"

It wasn't the first time he'd heard her refer to his wardrobe as death garb. Nor was it the first time he'd heard the lecture about the Church being an evil embarrassment to Christianity – her Christianity. Her view was the only view. Here she was reminding him, once again, why their relationship had faltered. "Mom, let's not get into our religious differences," he suggested, hoping to avoid a heated debate.

"It's my obligation, stemming from my love of God first, that I remind you of the passage from 2 Corinthians, *'that the god of this world has blinded the minds of the unbelievers, to keep them from seeing the light of the gospel of the glory of Christ, who is the image of God.'* I know you mean well son, you are a good boy, a gentle boy, and I have done everything I could do to save you from the fate of hell."

"Mother, please. The Catholic Church is not following the god of this world. We believe in the same God as you. The same Christ as you." He didn't want to have this debate.

But it was too late. His mother's tirade had begun. "Followers of my God are committed to developing Christ-like loving relationships and to keeping the unity of the Spirit by resolving our differences in a way that brings praise to God and leads others to know His infinite love. Followers of my God are not men who hide behind cloaks and lay with young boys." Her voice quivered at the indignity of it all. "Those are the men of your Church, Stephen; an evil omen of history repeating itself; Sodom and Gomorrah – the life to come should you stay amongst those misled by the god of the world."

Father Mario sighed deeply. This was the foundation of his relationship with his mother, an endless debate on belief. It wasn't so bad when he was growing up; but it was the only thing he had heard after giving his life to the Catholic Church – the endless barrage of condemnation. All to hell. According to his mother, very few would make it through the pearly gates, and never a Catholic. He knew his mother was a woman blinded by her own vision of the world and that he would never make headway with her.

Suddenly, his desire to see her had dissolved into a pathetic apathy. Yet, in spite of her faults, he could not see his mother as some rampaging murderess. Sure, she may be a little over-zealous, but not a schizophrenic, homicidal maniac. "Well, I hope you and Aunt Flora enjoy your time together and that your trip back home is safe," he finally offered, letting his mother know that, once again, she had built a wall between them that he didn't have the energy or ability to scale.

"Just remember, Stephen, everything I say and do is only meant to help you find everlasting peace. As your mother, I consider it my personal responsibility to my Master to do whatever I can to ensure you find the path to heaven. I love you, son. Everything I say and do is only out of my love for you."

I'm more at peace without your love, he thought sadly as he hung up the phone.

CHAPTER FIFTY-SIX

Chief Johnson stood before a small podium in front of the police station. He recognized most of the faces from the local television stations and press. Front and center was Julia, holding her iPhone, ready to record.

He cleared his throat and looked evenly into the nearest camera. "On Tuesday, July 19, at 0200 hours the dispatcher received a call from an unknown source reporting a disturbance at the Allen Conner residence on Mimosa Crescent. When officers arrived at the home, they discovered that Allen Conner, his wife Carol and their three children Michael, Patrick and James had been shot and were deceased. We do consider this a homicide and our investigations have uncovered a probable suspect who is still at large.

The suspect is identified as Constance Franklin Mario, who has been going by the name Ruth Christian. Ms. Mario is also wanted in Quanah, Texas, where she resided until about eight months ago, as a possible murder suspect. The suspect, who according to DMV records is 60 years old, was last known to be wearing a silver colored wig, shoulder-length with bangs. The suspect is thought to be driving a 1998 Green Mercury Sable station wagon.

It is also believed that the suspect took the family dog, a black cocker spaniel named Calvin, who has since been found in Dillon, South Carolina. The suspect is considered to be in South Carolina or possibly traveling into Georgia or Florida. She is considered armed and dangerous. Photos of the suspect, with and without the silver wig, are being released as we speak." Chief Johnson held up two photos for the cameras.

"We are asking all citizens who may have any knowledge of Ms. Mario's whereabouts to contact us immediately," Chief Johnson concluded. "At this time, I'll answer any questions."

"What's the motive for the suspect to murder an entire family?" came the first question from the local NBC station.

"It's too soon to say. Next question."

"Is there any connection between the suspect and the Conner's parish priest? They share the same last name," Julia asked, quickly finding a hook that would keep the public engaged.

"As a matter of fact, Ms. Frank, the suspect is the mother of Father Stephen Mario, the parish priest at St. Joseph's. However, there is no evidence at this point to suggest that Father Mario was involved and he is cooperating with police in our search to locate her."

Suddenly, questions were coming in from all directions. Julia Frank had hit a nerve and she smiled knowingly and winked at the Chief.

"What led you to name the priest's mother as the suspect?"

called several voices.

"We have forensics to thank for that lead," Chief Johnson responded. "The suspect's DNA was discovered at the scene and then linked back to Texas where she was already a suspect."

"Is there any link between the murder in Texas and here?" asked the correspondent from ABC.

"None that seems evident. Any more questions?"

"Why would the murderer take the dog? That makes no sense," asked a reporter that the chief did not recognize.

"Without having apprehended the suspect and knowing her psychological state of mind, it's hard to say. Unfortunately for us, the dog doesn't respond to questioning." The chief smiled at the crowd, most of whom were shaking their heads at his attempt at humor. "Let me just conclude by saying, we are hard at work and I expect to have this case closed very soon."

As Chief Johnson left the small crowd and went back into the station, he could hear questions still being asked. He had given the press the most important information and right now his mind was on the ticking clock.

Inside the station, he checked in with Lieutenant Eaton, who was running every known search in an attempt to locate Constance Franklin Mario, aka Ruth Christian. Not surprised by the lack of information the search provided, he grabbed a copy of her two photos and headed toward his car. "Eaton, I want a couple of cars over at St. Joseph's asap. I don't want the media hounding that poor priest until I've had a chance to talk to him."

"On it, sir," the lieutenant replied.

Chief Johnson's first stop was Newport News, where he knocked on the door of the Hispanic woman who he and

Sergeant Walker had spoken to earlier in the morning. On the way, he practiced his little bit of Spanish so that he could ask the one question for which he needed an answer.

When she came to the door, he greeted her and then asked in broken Spanish if the photo he held was of the woman that bought her husband's car. She smiled and answered with a word he knew. "Sí."

His next stop was St. Joseph's Catholic Church. When Chief Johnson pulled into the parking lot, he saw two cruisers in the parking lot and two of his officers talking to several disgruntled reporters. He pulled in and hastily headed for the church.

When he found the door of the church locked, he headed around the side where he knew the rectory to be. The small, white cottage looked inviting with the hydrangea framing both sides of the front door in full bloom. It reminded him of boyhood summers at his grandmother's home in the Virginia countryside.

Father Mario didn't come to the door until the third series of knocks and when he opened the door, the Chief didn't know if the priest had been sleeping or had drunk too much communion wine. The startled look that came across the priest's face didn't escape the Chief's observation.

"Father Mario, I'm sorry to bother you again – just can't seem to get rid of me, can you?" he said, trying to ease the mood.

Father Mario's smile appeared tired and forced, but he opened the door and stepped back to invite the Chief into his home.

Chief Johnson stepped in and surveyed the rooms out of habit. "May I sit for a minute? I have something to show you."

Father Mario waved toward the kitchen table and the two men took seats opposite each other. The Chief placed a leather portfolio on the table and opened it to pull a photo from the left-side sleeve. "Do you recognize this woman?" he asked.

Father Mario picked the photo up from the table and looked closely. "I think I've seen her at church," he said, placing the photo back down on the table.

"Look more closely," the Chief suggested. "Cover up the hair and just focus on the face."

Father Mario did as he asked and within seconds his face revealed all that Chief Johnson had expected. "This can't be... It can't be the same woman! You're playing tricks on me!" Father Mario's voice was accusatory and disbelieving.

"Father Mario, was your mother Catholic?"

Father Mario hesitated before shaking his head in answer, telling the Chief what he already knew. He could feel his face flush as he worked hard to keep his emotions in check.

"How did she feel about the Catholic Church – or, should I say, how did she feel about you, being a priest in the Catholic Church?"

Father Mario thought about their conversation just a couple of hours ago. He wanted desperately to think of some positive affirmation she may have given him over the years; but there was nothing from which he could draw. He sighed deeply and looked at Chief Johnson with the heaviness of the world once again on his shoulders. "She was not particularly supportive," he said finally.

"Father Mario, do you know where we could find your mother?"

Am I really having this conversation, Father Mario asked himself. "She lives in Quanah, Texas, 104 Main Street – just like I told the investigator earlier this morning."

"It just so happens that this morning I spoke with Hardeman County Sheriff Danny Pickens. He said your mother left Quanah about eight months ago. Sold everything of any value and just took off. Were you aware of this?" The Chief's voice had taken a sharper edge to it – daring Father Mario to cover up any truth.

The priest's face showed the shock he felt at hearing this information. "No, I had no idea she had left," he finally stammered.

"Does the name Darius Cash mean anything to you?"

Father Mario considered for a moment, going back in his mind to growing up in Quanah. "I do remember a Mr. Darius from Quanah. He had a daughter about my age. We went to the same school. Why do you ask?"

"Let me finish asking the questions if you don't mind," the Chief stated matter-of-factly. *Besides, I'm on a roll*, he thought. "When was the last time you spoke with your mother?"

Father Mario looked at him with a steady gaze. He knew what the next question would be. "I spoke to her about two hours ago. And to answer your next question, she is staying with her sister in Aynor, South Carolina. Now, can you tell me what is going on here? What does all this mean?"

Chief Johnson considered the priest sitting across the table. He concluded that a priest's job was to look for the good in people, to believe in positive intent, to always be willing to forgive and forget. Unlike Father Mario, the Chief's job was just the opposite. He had to consider all the evil that any person might be capable of doing. He had to consider motive and although there may be times he could forgive, he could never forget. But his gut had always told him that Father Mario was not guilty of any wrongdoing. Interesting how, in proving his innocence, Father Mario gave them the most significant lead of all. And for those reasons, Chief Johnson told Father Mario everything he had learned and what he believed had occurred and why.

Chief Johnson believed that the threats Father Mario received had come from his mother who had hoped to frighten him out of the Church. He believed that when she left Quanah, she decided to secretly check in on him to confirm her doubts about the intentions of the Church. She disguised herself and always came into church late and left early – at least according to Sarah Pulley. When all the parishioners were approached about the special committee being formed, Father Mario's mother was eager to join to learn more. The accusations from the committee had confirmed her fears about her son and the Church.

"This is where things get interesting," the Chief said. "Instead of continuing to leave threatening messages for you to find, she became angry at those who led the accusations against you – the Conner family."

The Chief went on to hypothesize how, over time, his mother had been able to endear herself to the Conner family and offer to help Mrs. Conner out at home. Over the Fourth of July weekend, the Conners asked her to stay in their home and take care of Calvin, the family dog. It was then that she plotted out the murders.

"You see," he said. "Not only did she want revenge against the Conners for trying to humiliate you, she had to get rid of Michael, the older son, with whom she thought you were intimately involved. In some strange way, she probably thought she was helping you."

Father Mario sat speechless, his mind thinking back to his mother's last words from their earlier call: "Everything I say and do is only out of my love for you." When at last he spoke, he asked two questions.

"Do you think she's sick? How else could someone have done such things?"

Chief Johnson considered the possibility. *No,* he thought. *She's just determined to have things her way.* He had seen it all and after a while he accepted the fact that the majority of criminals are just narcissistic. Funny how people always wanted to place the blame on something uncontrollable – some obscure mental illness or possible brain tumor.

He knew that in truth, bad people were so damned selfish and self-centered they would stop at nothing to get what they wanted. He'd seen parents deliberately destroy the lives of their children out of jealousy; children deceive and rob aging parents out of all they owned and then leave them penniless, with nothing but a Social Security check that couldn't even cover basic living expenses. He'd seen uncles rape their underage nieces to 'show them how it's done'; and nephews con their ways into their aunties' wills just because it was easier than getting a job. What really blew his mind was how, in all these cases, the perpetrators always justified their actions.

No, Chief Johnson didn't think Constance Mario was sick. He thought she was evil who clothed herself in the disguise of God's good word. He believed that Constance Mario used the word of God to justify everything she had ever done. In fact, he was willing to bet that she would testify how she was doing the world a favor by getting rid of evil-minded, ill-doing people. But these were not the things he'd share with Father Mario, who watched him now waiting for some affirmation.

"It's always a possibility," the Chief finally remarked. "You just never know with these kinds of things."

CHAPTER FIFTY-SEVEN

The following day the funeral for Kevin Larson was held at St. Mark's Catholic Church. Jenny Larson couldn't bear having the service at St. Joseph's knowing that was where Kevin had ended his life. Bishop Grogan returned, as promised, and stood at the front of the church facing a small group of mourners.

"Dear friends and family," Bishop Grogan began, "on joyous occasions we gather in celebration. We unite in our happiness, which becomes contagious. Tragedy is similar. We unite in our despair, which casts its shadow over us all.

I did not have the privilege of knowing Kevin in life. But I feel I have come to know him very well in his death. In many ways Kevin was like every other teenager. He longed for friendship and he found that in his dearest friend, Michael Conner whom he tragically lost earlier this week. To suffer the loss of one's best friend is unthinkable. What makes the loss even greater is that Michael was Kevin's only friend. Kevin was shy and sensitive and his friendship with Michael anchored him.

Like other teenagers, Kevin longed for understanding and

acceptance. He knew he was different and that difference was not accepted. Even adults find themselves in deep despair when alienated; imagine how painful this must have been for a youth just coming into his adulthood? Therefore, Kevin spent most of his short life hiding under a veil of fear and persecution.

What I've learned about Kevin is that his heart was a heart in turmoil. While he had great love, he also had great sorrow. To know Kevin, to really know him, means we must understand the pain that made him who he was. It is this very pain that gives each of us a chance to become more understanding, more loving, more embracing of those who are not like us.

Kevin's pain can be heard in this poem he left behind and which, with his mother's permission, I share with you now."

I know not who I am, nor what
Only that my heart swells with love
When I see his face
His beautiful face

Loathing myself is not enough
Praying to God is not enough
To rid myself of this fate
Our fate

If only I could explain
If only I knew the right words
If only I could be understood
If only

Bishop Grogan paused, allowing the haunting words to hang in the air. "As humans, we tend to judge appearance and behavior. But, our Lord looks past those things and sees into each and every heart. Even though Kevin found his outside world unbearable, he knew that God loved him as he was. This loss, however tragic, gives us the chance to reflect.

To fully honor Kevin, I ask each and every one of you to consider how you love. Not how you love your best friends, but how you love those that are unlike you. How you love those whose behaviors don't mirror your own. If we are to live as Jesus, we must learn to look for the beautiful spirit of the divine in each and every person we encounter, be it the beggar on the street corner or the young man in the hallway that just got pushed against the lockers by a bunch of football players calling him fag.

I can't imagine a greater tragedy than a child taking their life because of rejection. The pain for the family members left behind is indescribable. The only thing that a family can do in such a case is carry on in the unending love and mercy of our heavenly God. Let us pray."

Father Mario sat in the back row of the church feeling emotional and confused. The picture that Bishop Grogan painted of Kevin and his tortured spirit was as if the Bishop had been eavesdropping on Father Mario's conversations with Kevin and Michael. Little did Father Mario know that Bishop Grogan was painting the picture of his own brother who, like Kevin, had ended his life thinking death was better than the alternative. In Bishop Grogan's eulogy of Kevin, he was eulogizing every young person who had ended life due to the pain of exclusion.

Father Mario couldn't help but think of the Conner family and especially of Michael and his mother's involvement in their murders. He thought that, given the rest of his life, he would never come to understand all that had happened in just four days' time.

There would be no local service for the Conner family. Allen Conner's parents had the bodies returned to Connecticut, where Allen had grown up. The Conner home had been turned over to an auctioneer who was going to sell off everything, minus a few mementos that the elder Conners' had requested the Chief's permission to take.

When the service was over, Father Mario made his way through the mourners to find Jenny. Her eyes were red and swollen with grief and when she saw Father Mario reaching out to embrace her, she allowed her tears to flow.

"I'm so sorry Father Mario. I hope you can forgive me."

He pulled away from the embrace and held her shoulders firmly. "Jenny, you don't owe me any apologies. I have failed you. I didn't have the right words to offer enough hope to Kevin. I hope you can forgive me."

"I've learned so much about Kevin in the last couple of days," she said. "And, other mothers have come forward to share their stories with me about their sons and daughters. After things have settled down a bit, I think I may become a parent advocate for gay teens. I may not have understood Kevin or been able to support him in the way he needed, but I might be able to help other parents understand what's at stake in situations like this."

"That's a wonderful legacy for Kevin," Father Mario responded. "It takes such strength on your part, Jenny."

She thanked him and then, with an embarrassed look, asked what he would do when things settled down.

Why should Father Mario think that the news of his mother's

arrest had not spread to the mourners here in the church? Everyone probably knew. Working with both the Dillon and Aynor police departments, his mother was picked up at his Aunt Flora's house. She was still wearing her silver wig.

The car she had arrived in was a green Mercury Sable. Inside the car, they found dog hair matching that from the Conner house and, most significantly, the murder weapons – an S&W, single-action, .22 double revolver and a Glock 9 mm. Her prints were on both guns and matched prints found in the house. All the evidence was there. She had been transported back to Hampton early this morning where she was jailed without bail. The trial date had not yet been set, but the arrest and her photo was all over the news – how could anyone not know?

Although he had not seen or spoken with his mother since yesterday's call, he was beginning to think Chief Johnson's theory was a possibility after all. His mother had sent threats to his church hoping to frighten him away. When she left Quanah eight months ago, she came to the area, but disguised herself and kept her distance so that he wouldn't recognize her.

When she had learned about the plot to oust him as the parish priest, she had joined, thinking that would be a way to have him leave the Church. Instead, she had grown angry with Allen Conner for his attack against her son and took retribution. She had successfully removed others who had gotten in her way. A husband who had abused her and her son. Darius Cash, a man who she had entrusted with her darkest secret. It had all seemed preposterous yesterday to hear Chief Johnson tell it; but now Father Mario was beginning to piece the truth together in his own mind.

"It's hard for me to say at this point," he said, his voice trembling. "But I think it's best for me to leave St. Joseph's and give the church family a better chance of healing."

"I trust you are looking for ways to heal yourself, too," Jenny offered, her eyes shedding new tears. "We all have to look for ways to heal; otherwise, what kind of life can we expect to live?" She turned toward Caroline who had slipped up from behind and slid her hand into her mother's. Mother and daughter exchanged teary-eyed smiles. "I have Caroline to live for and that is enough for me now. All you need to do is search deep in your heart and find what it is that makes your life worth living." Then, pulling Caroline's hand close to her heart, she turned to leave.

Father Mario watched as Jenny and Caroline walked out the door and into the July sun. In the distance he saw Kevin's father Larry pacing next to his parked car. Father Mario's heart sank at the pain Larry must be feeling and he wondered if Kevin's father could ever forgive himself for disowning his son just because he didn't fit into his vision of what a son should be.

He thought back to Kevin telling him how much he loved his father and wanted to please him, but that he didn't know how to do that and be the person that he was. Larry's rejection of Kevin had been harsh and emotionally scarring, not very different from the rejection Father Mario had suffered by his own mother.

Looking back inside, he saw Bishop Grogan speaking quietly to Father Cameron. There was no one else left inside the small church save one man sitting near the back. It took him a moment before he recognized Sergeant Walker, who was dressed in civilian clothes. The tall, dark-haired police officer was wiping tears from his eyes.

Father Mario turned away, pushed his hands deep into his pockets and rocked back and forth on his feet. He was searching for balance – some place safe from suffering and pain – a place where he could reflect on his life. He was searching for a place where, as Jenny had so wisely counseled, he could consider what made life worth living.

Realizing that life offered no place safe from suffering and pain, he recalled the verse written hundreds of years before Christ by the Greek Aeschylus:

He who learns must suffer.
And even in our sleep, pain that cannot forget
falls drop by drop upon the heart,
and, in our own despair, against our will,
comes wisdom to us
by the awful grace of God.

Glancing once last time into the church, Father Mario's eyes met Bishop Grogan's and for a brief moment he felt reassured. Then, turning toward the door he walked out into the heat of the July sun.

RESOURCES

Lesbian, gay, bisexual, transgender and questioning (LGBTQ) youth are up to four times more likely to attempt suicide than their heterosexual peers, according to the Massachusetts 2006 Youth Risk Survey. A 2009 study, "Family Rejection as a Predictor of Negative Health Outcomes" conducted as part of the Family Acceptance Project at San Francisco State University, shows that adolescents who were rejected by their families for being LGBT were 8.4 times more likely to report having attempted suicide.

In "Always Our Children" the Catholic Church urges parents of questioning and GLBT children to love and accept them, citing, "God does not love someone any less simply because he or she is homosexual. God's love is always and everywhere offered to those who are open to receiving it."
http://nccbuscc.org/laity/always.shtml

A few additional resources for LGBTQ youth and the families and friends who love them include:

- The Trevor Project operates the only accredited, nationwide, around-the-clock crisis and suicide prevention helpline for LGBTQ youth.
  http://www.thetrevorproject.org/
- Parents, Families and Friends of Lesbians and Gays (PFLAG) is a national non-profit organization providing information about sexual orientation and gender identity. Find your local community on their website. http://community.pflag.org/
- It Gets Better is a website where LGBTQ youth have

access to more than 10,000 inspirational videos, created to help those who feel excluded on the basis of sexual orientation understand that life is always worth living. http://www.itgetsbetter.org